โขนข้างแคร่

Story : Teerinthorn | illus : PAUOON

Khon
Spy behind the Fallen Prince

STORY: **Teerinthorn**

Editor: **Niphon Thiangtham**

Illustrator: **Pauoon**

Genres: **A historical romance with LGBTQ+ themes**

paperback – 979-8-9937656-0-0

hardcover – 979-8-9937656-1-7

Award: **Long list Writer Zeed 4 2023**

Dedication

To Chanit Bhukanchana, my father and my first teacher,

You placed a book in my hands and a dream in my heart to be a true writer. For every lesson, every chance, and every door you opened, this work is my step forward because you believed in me.

Acknowledgment

My heartfelt thanks to Khru Niphon Thiangtham whose guidance, wisdom, and unyielding dedication shaped this novel into something magnificent. His feedback echoed in my ears, and through it I learned what it truly means to write fiction.

Thank you to Oxford Publishing for producing and preparing the English edition with care and professionalism.

And to the many teachers who offered encouragement, read drafts, and shared invaluable historical insights. Your support made this journey possible.

Contents

Dedication iii

Acknowledgment iv

Chapter 1 1

Chapter 2 30

Chapter 3 49

Chapter 4 74

Chapter 5 100

Chapter 6 118

Chapter 7 135

Chapter 8 156

Chapter 9 168

Chapter 10 173

Chapter 11 190

Chapter 12 205

Chapter 13 218

Chapter 14 229

Chapter 15 236

Chapter 16 252

Chapter 17 264

Chapter 18 276

Chapter 1

Following the death of King Rama II, the legitimate heir, who later became King Rama IV, was still a very young child. At a time when Western colonial powers were rapidly expanding into Asia, many feared that a child monarch might be unable to safeguard the kingdom.

To mitigate this risk, **Prince Khun Luang**, the King's younger brother, advocated for the King's eldest son, the child of his principal wife from before his accession, to ascend the throne instead.

The plan succeeded, and Prince Khun Luang became the most powerful aristocrat in Siam, wielding immense influence behind the throne.

***

Early Rattanakosin Era

On the full moon night of the sixth month, Year of the Ox, 1191 BE.

The aching sobs swept through the golden teak house, heavy as the season's first storm rising off the Bang Luang Canal. Thien knelt silently beside the lady of the house. He was only seven years old, yet the memory of that night forged the purpose he bore all his days.

Thien woke early that morning, bathed, and sat still as his servant styled his hair into a tidy topknot. He donned a carefully pleated purple jongkaben and a floral-printed shirt. For once, he wore the shirt without protest as his adoptive father had promised to take him to the market for a birthday gift, a Western custom that thrilled him.

Once dressed, he ran to the pier in front of the house and nestled beside his adoptive mother, Mhom Jan. Together, they gazed out at the river, the air heavy with morning mist.

"Nimon, please come," Mhom Jan said softly, inviting the monk who arrived with his disciple. Before long, a small rowing boat docked. Thien picked up a long-stemmed lotus flower, waiting for his mother to scoop warm rice and several side dishes into the alms bowl. Then, he stepped forward and gently placed the lotus on top of the lid before joining hands and bowing his head slightly to receive the monk's blessing chant.

After the final chant, the disciple dipped his oars into the water, guiding the vessel gently away from the pier. As Mhom Jan moved to rise, her arm brushed the offering tray. The Benjarong porcelain lid slipped from the edge and struck the teak floor with a sharp crack.

She froze. Her gaze fell to the broken porcelain, eyes darkening with unease. The air seemed suddenly too quiet. His mother's fingers tighten, just for a moment. Although to him, it had seemed like nothing—a minor accident.

Thien finished his meal in haste. The morning sun slanted across the floor of the riverside pavilion as he played with his marbles. He flicked them across the boards, pausing every time he heard oars or footsteps. As the sun climbed higher, his excitement began to fade. By noon, he sat still, knees tucked under his chin.

The house was quiet. Mhom Jan's bedroom doors were

shut. He made his way to the library, where the scriptures of Chindamani lay open. Dipping the brush into ink, he traced each curve until his eyes grew heavy, and sleep gently claimed him.

He woke to the soft footsteps of a man with a familiar figure, dressed in a white shirt and a silken royal court wrap folded high above the knees. He was one of his father's trusted men.

Silently, Mhom Jan stepped into the room. The man bowed low before her.

"Forgive my intrusion, Mhom," he said, voice low. "The master. He has been taken…"

She didn't reply. Her hand halted midair, and her face turned ashen, eyes frozen in disbelief.

"for spreading seditious letters."

Thien stood behind the doorframe, unseen. His thoughts drifted back to the morning. Suddenly, he understood Mhom Jan's unease.

It was not a regular accident. The broken porcelain lid. A bad omen. She must have sensed something was wrong from the moment his father left the house.

Khon Spy Behind the Fallen Prince

The lady of the house sat weeping on the wooden bench, her shoulders shaking as tears streamed down her face. Around her, servants sobbed in shared sorrow. When she saw Thien bowing nearby, she opened her arms and drew him close, clutching him tightly as though he were all she had left.

Rumors quickly spread that the royal court was searching for the author of the slanderous letters against the princes. Police were arresting suspects all over the city. Thien's father was among them, now imprisoned in the royal jail with an uncertain fate.

Thien was overcome with sorrow, able to do nothing but weep beside his mother through the long hours of the night. Even the household slaves were moved to tears by the depth of their anguish.

Under the pale gaze of the full moon, Thien knelt in silence, vowing that one day, he would make those who accused his father pay.

10 Years Later

The steady tapping of wooden sticks echoed through the

hall, mixing with the stamp of heels on the floor. Master Boonsri sat with his knees up, clapping along to the rhythm, his eyes bright with pride as he watched his favorite student practicing the dance move.

Thien's topknot was long gone, but his smooth face still held the softness of youth. His long double eyelids, naturally red lips, and fair skin stood out against his dark, arched brows—features that reminded one of a Portuguese painting.

"If you keep dancing like this," Master Boonsri said, his voice low but firm, "you'll soon take the lead role at the royal troupe of Prince Khun Luang."

The words struck Thien deeply. Tears pricked at the corners of his eyes. Soon, he would have to leave the place where he had lived and trained for ten years since the day his father died behind prison walls.

"What now? If you don't want to go, you're welcome to stay. I don't really want to send you away either, you know." Master Boonsri gave a small laugh to ease the boy's sorrow, though he knew Thien's heart was already set on revenge.

Thien said nothing. He only bowed low, accepting the

praise, and wiped at his tears, doing his best to hold back the sob building in his chest.

"Going there will do you good. Prince Khun Luang's Khon troupe is as magnificent as his rank demands. The theater is lavishly adorned, and the dancers wear ornaments crafted by royal artisans. It's a world apart from performing before temples or in brothels."

"Have you ever watched the women dance in the Sampheng brothels?" Thien teased, his voice still shaky with emotion.

"Y-You little rascal! Get over here. Let me smack that head of yours!" Master Boonsri snapped, pretending to reach for a stick. But Thien knew he would never actually strike him.

Everyone in the troupe knew that Thien was the master's favorite because he was the adoptive son of their patron, who had supported Master Boonsri since the troupe's early days.

As his true goal was to avenge his father's death, Thien had been sent to study the fundamentals of dance under Master Boonsri's guidance by KhunPhraNai Sakdiphon, a former confidant of his father who now promoted to head of the royal pages. It was also him who arranged for Thien to train with the prince's Khon troupe.

"Ah, there's KhunPhraNai now," said the master, pointing to the approaching figure. The two men greeted each other before KhunPhraNai turned to Thien.

"Ready, Thien?"

Although they had spoken only a few times, Thien felt more at ease with KhunPhraNai than with most nobles. He was friendly and approachable, often spending quiet evenings with Thien's father over cups of rice wine. So when he asked Thien for help, Thien agreed without hesitation.

"Yes, I'm ready." He grabbed his cloth bag, slung it over one shoulder, and gave a deep bow to Master Boonsri, who had trained him for years and treated him like a second son. Since Thien rarely returned to his mother's house except for short visits, this place had long felt like home.

After leaving the dance school, KhunPhraNai took Thien to pay respects to LuangTa Phu, a former noble who had served the previous king before becoming a monk. The monk blessed him, boosting his confidence for the mission ahead.

Only a handful of people knew that Thien was a spy, sent to infiltrate the Khon troupe of Khun Luang, a prince famed for both his immense power and his complicated reputation.

Thien wasn't sure what tasks lay ahead, having never met the prince before. He knew only that the prince was involved in his father's imprisonment. This knowledge alone drove him to leave his mother's home without hesitation.

"Make yourself trustworthy but not too conspicuous. I'll send further instructions later," KhunPhraNai advised as he noticed Thien wiping sweat from his palms.

Thien wasn't afraid for himself. What truly terrified him was the thought of failure and the danger it would bring to everyone connected to the mission. One wrong move could bring everything crashing down. The punishment for a failed spy was death by whipping: slow, brutal, and intended to serve as an example.

***

The long-tail boat bobbed gently along the canal, a hush of anticipation swelling within Thien as the narrow waterway opened into the broad, glistening stretch of the Chao Phraya

River. He leaned forward, his eyes wide, his heart quickening at the sight of the Grand Palace rising above the banks, its gilded spires gleaming beside the graceful silhouettes of beautiful pagodas. It was just as people said, a dwelling fit for gods and heavenly maidens, a true abode of the divine.

He had never seen anything like it.

The Khon Dance Academy of Prince Khun Luang was located just beyond the palace walls. At the front stood a large theater with white plastered walls and a roof covered in gleaming Chinese tiles. Next to the theater stretched a long row of classrooms built in the traditional Thai style. The walls were polished teak, the slanted roofs adorned with wooden eaves carved in delicate patterns. Open verandas surrounded the structure, where potted plants were neatly arranged to bring a touch of greenery before each doorway. Bright curtains fluttered at the windows, while the scent of freshly varnished wood mingled with the fragrance of jasmine drifting on the breeze.

The Khon troupe members' eyes followed Thien as he arrived. It had been years since a new student had joined. Master Maan introduced himself and then took Thien on a tour of the Khon dance academy and the teachers' residence.

There was one place Master Maan didn't take him inside. They only walked past it. It was a golden teak house at the far right near the pier, known to the dancers as Ruen Horton. The house stood tall on wooden stilts, with several steps leading up to a shaded veranda. It used to be the private residence of Prince Khun Luang, whom everyone here respectfully called *Sadet Chaokhana*, meaning 'Master Prince.'

"Back in the early days, students used to practice dancing at Ruen Horton," Master Maan said gently. "But once more students joined, Sadet Chaokhana built a proper theater. So his old house became a library and occasionally a guest house for foreign visitors." He spoke with the calm tone of someone passing down a bit of history, then quietly returned Thien to KhunPhraNai for their farewell.

KhunPhraNai discreetly handed Thien a piece of paper, which he opened after Master Maan left.

"If not necessary, don't contact me. I will reach out to you," the paper read, providing the address of a small pharmacy in Thonburi.

The secret code was clear: "Complain of uneasiness and

sleeplessness, needing medicine to sleep. I will visit at dusk."

Thien nodded slowly in understanding.

***

The new Khon dance master was kind and gentle, with a thick mustache and a slightly stout figure. Yet when performing female roles, he moved with surprising grace, as if weightless, with elegance in every gesture.

He was nothing like Prince Khun Luang, the troupe's formidable patron. The prince was known for his loud voice and sudden mood swings. On some days, he was all charm and generosity. On others, he was as fearsome as a demon king with ten heads and twenty arms, utterly unapproachable and impossible to please.

Besides practicing dance, the Khon dancers also contributed to the academy's daily upkeep. They swept the stage, prepared costumes, and even assisted with documents and finances. Only the kitchen and housework were left to the permanent servants.

Among the many performers, two stood out. They stood out in ways that sparked both praise and jealousy.

The first was Singh. The junior members called him 'Inao'. He played the lead role in almost every performance and served as the head student, keeping a strict watch over the others. He made sure no one broke the rules or acted out of line. Anyone wishing to leave the academy had to report to him. Leaving without permission was strictly forbidden.

The other was Plang, known by all as 'Busaba', a name borrowed from the graceful heroin he often portrayed onstage. Though he was a man, Plang embraced the character so completely that the name clung to him, a second skin he wore with delight whenever someone called him Busaba. His delicate mannerisms, paired with a sharp wit, lent him a charm few could resist.

Acting as the prince's scribe, he alone had free access to Ruen Horton. Anyone wishing to send a message to the prince had to go through him.

Inao and Busaba could not have been more different from each other. Inao was stern but fair, a figure who commanded both respect and awe. Busaba, on the other hand, was all sweetness on the surface, flattering, graceful, and often dressed like a court lady. At royal events, he sometimes accompanied the prince in full Khon costume, so convincing that he was often mistaken for a royal consort. He always stayed close, attentive to the prince's every word and glance, his posture refined yet unmistakably possessive. It was no secret to anyone that he guarded his place beside the prince with a simmering pride.

Unfortunately for Thien, he had been assigned to study female roles, which meant he would have constant contact with Busaba. For reasons unknown, Busaba seemed to detest him, as if holding an old grudge. Every time Master Maan praised Thien, Busaba would tilt his head slightly, folding his hands as if in agreement. Then came the soft voice, perfectly measured.

"Oh? That gesture again? How charming," he would say with a delicate smile. "Though I must admit, it still lacks the softness of silk. Perhaps it's his youth and inexperience or the lack of a proper foundation." He never raised his voice. His words floated like scented smoke, pleasant at first, the sting lingering long after.

Despite Master Maan's consistent praise for Thien's grace and quick learning, he never interrupted Busaba's remarks. Now and then, his lips would tighten, or his fingers pause mid-beat, but he said nothing. To contradict Busaba in front of others was to risk drawing the prince's attention. Besides, some battles were best left unfought.

That did not mean Thien never caught a glimpse of the troupe's master. Sometimes, he saw the prince passing by the classrooms and would bow respectfully from a distance. At other times, in the quiet of dawn, he glimpsed him from the pier when the prince stepped out to wash his face at the veranda. Thien often rose before sunrise to secure the bathing spot early, hoping to avoid sharing it with the others.

After several weeks of brief, silent glances, the prince finally descended and asked Thien his name.

"Your Highness, my name is Thien. I was granted the honor of joining the troupe through the kindness of KhunPhraNai Sakdiphon." Thien quickly straightened himself into a kneeling posture and bowed his head respectfully.

The prince fell silent for a moment, offering no reply. He looked at the young man once more, then turned and ascended the steps back to his quarters.

Thien pressed his palms together in a 'wai', the customary Thai bow of respect, and let out a quiet breath, relieved that no one had witnessed the exchange. Especially since Busaba was not an early riser, had he seen it, Thien would surely have earned one of his sharp glares, as if to say, 'How bold of you to place yourself before Sadet Chaokhana without my permission.'

***

Thien had been at the academy for over three months before he found himself interacting with Prince Khun Luang beyond mere formal greetings.

One morning, as the Khon dancers rehearsed in the grand hall, the prince descended from his quarters and walked past the rows of male performers. He paused before the group portraying female roles. These dancers, though all male, were trained to move with the delicate grace of court ladies, every gesture refined and precise. The prince's gaze lingered, focused and silent.

Busaba smiled to himself, certain he had caught the prince's attention. He alone wore a powdered white face and crimson lips, moving with practiced elegance. In that moment, he was the very image of classical grace.

The prince leaned in and whispered something to Master Maan.

Khon Spy Behind the Fallen Prince

A moment later, Master Maan clapped his hands once, sharply. "Stop." Then, with a courteous nod toward the prince, Master Maan added, "We have many new students this year, Your Highness." His gaze shifted past Busaba and settled on Thien.

Realizing his mistake, Busaba's expression stiffened.

"Thien." Master Maan called out.

Upon hearing his name, he crawled forward on his knees and bowed low at the prince's feet.

Though said to be past forty, Prince Khun Luang bore none of the wear that age might suggest. His face was smooth and finely sculpted, with high cheekbones and sharp, commanding eyes that gleamed like obsidian beneath arched brows. His complexion, fair and clear, caught the morning light like polished ivory. A faint smile played on his lips, as if he saw more than he let on.

He stood tall and straight, his broad shoulders draped in finely woven silk. At his waist hung a ceremonial sword with a gold-embossed hilt. There was an ease in the way he carried himself, elegant yet powerful. Every step seemed measured, every gesture precise.

Thien began to understand why Busaba held the prince so dearly, as though he were not a master to serve, but a possession too precious to share.

"Let me see the dance 'Busaba Sieng Thien'," the prince said, his tone calm yet commanding.

At the signal, the musicians struck a slow, lingering note. Thien stepped forward, his bare feet gliding across the polished floor. With arms lifted and fingers gently curved, he traced invisible patterns through the air. Every movement was deliberate yet fluid, as if he were painting emotion with his body.

Master Maan often praised Thien for his graceful form and quick grasp of the art. What he never realized was that such elegance had been forged through years of punishing discipline under Master Boonsri, who wrenched his legs apart and struck his ankles until they darkened with bruises. Every blow, every ache, was part of a design laid long ago, a preparation for the day Thien would strike at the shadowed powers within the royal palace.

The boy knew that to earn the prince's notice, he would have to rise above the rest. Now, before the court's watchful eyes, Thien danced with poise and precision. But even perfection did not silence Busaba.

"His feet barely rooted. See how he totters?" Busaba's lips curled into a smile too sweet to be sincere.

Master Maan's face tightened. He had held his tongue many times before, but not today.

"Not everyone is born flawless, like you are." Master Maan let out a soft sigh, finally losing patience. Despite his usual tolerance, he could not ignore such blatant criticism in front of the prince. "He's trained for less than a year. Yet even so, he's come this far."

"Training for less than a year. Impressive! Next month is the birthday celebration of Sia Lu Ma' mother. He's the silk merchant from China. His shop isn't far from the Grand Palace. Master Maan, prepare three or four Khon pieces. Let Thien perform alongside Plang. Ensure the dancers are dressed in their finest regalia. Sia Lu Ma has never seen a fully costumed Khon performance, and I want to show him that our troupe can be just as grand as any Chinese opera." The prince was pleased to have found a promising new Khon dancer.

These days, Khon performances based on royal court

scripts were in high demand. Traditionally, Khon had been performed exclusively within the palace, earning the name Lakhon Nai, or "inner court theatre." The dancers followed meticulously crafted verses written by court poets, Khon masters, and even former kings and princes, adhering to the refined standards of royal performance. But things changed. After the king banned all forms of entertainment inside the palace, Khon was thrust onto the public stage. What had once been a royal secret became something the people outside could finally see.

Even though it had left the palace walls, it kept its charm. The dancers still wore glittering jewels and full regalia, and every movement was polished and elegant. It was a far cry from the loud, lewd gestures found in common folk plays. Most villagers had never seen anything like it and were immediately captivated. Still, only the wealthy, like Sia Lu Ma, could afford to host such performances at home. They would set up private theaters with silk backdrops and invite guests to witness the splendor up close.

What made it even more ironic was that many former lakhon nai dancers, who once sneered at public shows as "commoners' plays," now had to join outside troupes just to survive. In a turn of fate, they were laughed at by the same people they had once looked down on. Some were so ashamed that they gave up performing altogether and never returned to the stage.

Thien, who had never danced on either a royal stage or a public one, felt both nervous and excited. Next month will be his first time before a real audience. He told himself he had to train harder than ever, if only to keep Busaba from finding another excuse to mock him.

***

Thien's debut on stage was anything but smooth. Even before the performance began, unease had already set in. The makeup artist worked with a tight-lipped expression, brushing powder onto his face without care. It was clear she had no intention of making him look his best, perhaps because she feared he might outshine Busaba.

Backstage was no better. Whispers buzzed like mosquitoes around him. Every time he passed by, conversations hushed or shifted. He caught words like "newcomer" and "too soon" hanging in the air. Some dancers looked through him, while others threw glances sharp enough to pierce skin.

Thien tried to focus on his training, on the months of

practice and the pain he had endured to reach this point. Yet the noise, both around him and inside his head, was deafening. His palms felt clammy. His breath caught in his chest. He kept adjusting his costume even when it didn't need fixing.

It wasn't that he lacked confidence. He knew the steps, and he had rehearsed until his muscles could move on their own. But something about today —the tension in the air and the eyes that watched him not with hope but with judgment —made his knees feel less steady and his heartbeat too loud.

"You seem troubled," said a gentle voice behind him. "That's natural. The first time always makes you nervous. Picture the audience as statues in a garden. They won't notice if you slip. They've never seen a court dance before."

Thien turned, surprised to see Prince Khun Luang standing behind him. "Your Highness noticed?" he asked, unable to hide the edge in his voice. He inhaled slowly, trying to calm the stirrings in his chest.

"It's not the dance I'm afraid of, Your Highness," he said at last. "It's the noise. The whispers. The ones who wait for me to stumble."

The prince tilted his head, his gaze thoughtful.

"You mean Busaba?"

"Your Highness noticed?" Thien is unable to keep the edge from his voice. "If Busaba were not your favorite, I doubt he would dare speak so freely about me."

The prince offered a quiet smile, undisturbed by Thien's candor. "Favor must be earned," he said, voice gentle but firm. "If you perform well tonight, I shall ensure you are properly rewarded."

"A reward, Your Highness? I am merely doing what is expected of any Khon dancer."

"Indeed," the prince replied. "And should you make no mistake, you will be more than merely expected. That is when merit begins."

With that, the prince returned to his seat before the stage, leaving Thien alone to compose himself. Those few graceful yet resolute words sparked something in Thien. As he stepped onto the stage, the chatter and stares faded. Each movement he performed was deliberate and assured, not a single gesture out of place.

The same students who had once whispered that he had advanced only through Master Maan's favor now approached him with praise. Even Sia Lu Ma, the silk merchant hosting the celebration, commented on the elegance of his dance and awarded him a sum equal to Busaba's.

Busaba, however, could not mask his displeasure. His painted lips tightened, his cheeks flushed with indignation. He let out a sharp "hmph" before leaving the stage without a word.

Later, after paying his respects to the host, Thien went in search of Prince Khun Luang, hoping to speak with him again. A servant directed him to the guest lounge, where the prince was enjoying tea and tobacco.

As Thien approached the lounge, he stopped just short of the door. Laughter drifted out, light and elegant, and it was Busaba's voice. He sounded as sweet as sugar in tea, giggling softly as he praised himself with well-practiced modesty.

Yet the sweetness quickly turned to gossip. In the same honeyed tone, he began to pick apart those around him. Singh, his longtime partner on stage, was "too stiff to be Inao." Another dancer "lacked discipline." The rest were "not ready for real court performances." He spoke as if merely chatting, never raising his voice, never sounding angry, but every remark carried the sting of mockery, cutting into his companions' reputations.

Thien listened, a knot forming in his chest. He should have expected this. Busaba wore his charm like stage makeup, flawless under candlelight but false all the same. People admired his grace, his elegance, his beauty. But they did not see the rot beneath, or perhaps they did and chose not to care.

What a shame, Thien thought. To be so beautiful, and yet so petty.

Thien lowered his hand, no longer inclined to knock. He turned back and returned to sit among the other performers, his earlier excitement now replaced with disappointment.

This was the world he had entered, and the mission he carried. With Busaba's shadow cast so wide, he wondered how long it would take before he could finally see his revenge fulfilled.

***

In addition to his training and scheduled performances, Thien was assigned clerical work such as keeping documents in order and occasionally assisting with the Khon troupe accounts. His sharp eyes and strong literacy skills made him especially suited to the role. At the long desks, he often worked beside Yot, another Khon dancer who had spent years at the academy yet had never once been chosen to perform.

"Yot's never been cast because he's lazier than a water buffalo," Master Maan would say. He was not the kind of man who enjoyed gossip, but whenever he scolded someone, his words were direct and to the point. Nobody ever felt offended, for his rebukes carried no cruelty. Being corrected by him felt more like learning a lesson than being punished.

"Oh, Master, my arms are stiff and my legs clumsy. I'd rather play music! When will you let me try the ranat?" Yot would complain half in jest, his whining always earning a laugh from those nearby.

"You can't even remember dance steps, and now you want to hit the ranat? Give me a break," Master Maan muttered, shaking his head before storming off as if the mere thought had insulted his ears.

The dormitory for Khon dancers was divided into small

rooms, usually housing two or three people. Never four. Master Maan considered the number inauspicious. Every time four students shared a room, fights inevitably broke out, and someone had to be moved.

Thien was placed in a room with Yot, as both were tasked with accounting duties. Master Maan figured they could help keep each other on schedule. The room had initially housed Yot and Boonmak, a Ranat player born in the Front Palace, whose mother had served as a lady-in-waiting. He had been training in music since childhood. With Thien joining them, the trio made use of the room's larger size, which had once been a rehearsal space for musicians.

There weren't many women in the academy. Most were related to the house servants or were distant kin of Master Maan himself. Even so, he didn't train female dancers, having spent his life coaching men in the Khon tradition. He also wanted to avoid the complications of romance in the academy.

Not that such complications were completely absent.

"You ever notice how Muang keeps looking at me?" Yot whispered one day, mid-stretch, as he helped Thien loosen his legs. Daily stretching was essential for maintaining the flexibility of a Khon dancer.

Muang, Master Maan's niece, was only twelve and still wore her hair in a traditional topknot.

Thien didn't even look. Master Maan had made it crystal clear: any romantic entanglement in the troupe would be met with immediate expulsion. And Muang, being the niece of the master, would make any transgression twice as dangerous.

"There! She's looking at me again!" Yot puffed his chest, proudly showing off his skinny arms, only to freeze when Muang actually walked toward them. Even Thien looked up, stunned.

"Yot, may I speak with you for a moment?" she asked, eyes lowered and cheeks red as she tugged her shawl and led him aside. Yot flashed Thien a triumphant grin before following. But he returned not long after, sulking.

"What happened?" Thien raised an eyebrow.

"She asked what food you like," Yot grumbled. "She said you danced beautifully at Sia Lu Ma's event and wanted to cook something special for you."

Muang's mother ran the kitchen, and Muang often helped,

learning to cook from an early age.

"There are plenty of good dancers," Yot muttered, shooting Thien a bitter look. "She never offered to cook for any of them."

He sighed deeply. "Why couldn't I have been born with a face like yours? The girls in this troupe go on and on about how pretty you are. Even Muang's fallen for you."

Thien burst out laughing, showing no sympathy. Yot looked ready to kick him and actually raised a foot in mock-threat, prompting Thien to hold up a hand in surrender.

"Don't worry," Thien said. "I'm not looking for love. I'm an orphan—no home to return to. If I get kicked out of here, I've got nowhere else to go. I'm not about to risk it all chasing romance."

That wasn't a lie. But he also never mentioned being the adopted son of a nobleman. With the palace rife with factional tension, one could never be sure who stood with whom. Better to keep one's secrets to oneself.

Chapter 2

After that night's performance, the prince did not return to the Khon academy for several months. His Majesty the King had ordered him, along with other royals, to suppress the opium trade at the Siamese border.

Opium had become a national crisis, spreading even into the capital. Some greedy nobles and officials were secretly trading it within the palace. The King, furious, vowed severe punishment. A royal decree urged anyone hiding opium to confess in exchange for clemency. Confiscated opium was burned publicly before Sutthasawan Hall.

When the mission was complete, Prince Khun Luang returned to visit Busaba and the Khon troupe. On that day, he was seated before the stage in the theatre. The vast hall lay in silence.

Around him sat only a handful of performers in a loose circle; their splendid costumes had been set aside, leaving them in the plain attire worn after rehearsal.

Here, within the emptiness of the theatre, he spoke not of dance or music. His voice carried instead the weight of state affairs. The performers listened closely as he addressed matters of law and dispute, particularly one case.

A fire had broken out in Sampheng (Chinatown). The accused was Choi, the daughter of a senior official who had served the previous monarch, King Rama II, Prince Khun Luang's father. Though noble-born, she had been sold to a brothel by her father and his wife, who resented her beauty.

The fire, she claimed, started as she fought off a Chinese guard. Due to the crowded layout of Sampheng, it spread rapidly. The case reached court with major claims for damages. The prince raised the matter because Choi was the sister of Cheua, one of the Khon dancers.

"The evidence is clear, isn't it?" the prince said. "Choi confessed to spilling the oil lamp. Then she must pay for the damages."

Though of noble blood, Choi had no allies. Born to a servant mother and abandoned, her beauty had brought her only scorn. She insisted the fire was an accident during a struggle.

"She didn't mean to start the fire. It was an accident, Your Highness," Cheua pleaded, bowing low at the prince's feet. He could only appeal for mercy; he had no bribes to offer, unlike Busaba, who had been subtly trying to sway the prince's judgment. Her words came like a rehearsed script, urging the prince to side with the noble family and place the blame squarely on Choi.

Thien listened in silence, pitying Choi. Without the means to pay the fine, she would likely face life in prison or something worse.

"And you," the prince turned suddenly to Thien and asked. "What do you think?"

Busaba shot Thien a warning glance, his expression sharp.

"Your Highness, I've heard whispers that the Lantern House is tied to opium smugglers. Perhaps the fire provides sufficient reason to take a closer look. It may reveal more than just negligence." Thien took no side, but subtly opened a door to

Khon Spy Behind the Fallen Prince

justice and opportunity.

The prince nodded slowly.

"You're Thien, aren't you?"

"Yes, Your Highness," Thien answered, bowing respectfully.

"I never did reward you for your performance at Sia Lu Ma's celebration. Here is my offer. If I can uncover concrete evidence of opium trafficking at the Lantern House, I will double your reward." The prince's voice rang with excitement, for he saw a chance not merely to kill two birds with one stone but to bring down an entire flock.

Busaba's jaw slackened in disbelief, and he rolled his eyes in his usual display of disdain. Thien, by contrast, barely blinked. He had grown too accustomed to Busaba's theatrics. With a bow, he left the stage before anyone else. A faint smirk tugged at his lips.

At last, a new path opened before Thien, one that might lead straight to the heart of his enemy.

***

Days later, Prince Khun Luang led a raid that shook the quarter awake. Soldiers stormed through shuttered doors and overturned furniture until the truth revealed itself: crates of opium, stacked and hidden beneath floorboards and false walls. The air reeked of dust and bitter smoke as, one by one, the contraband caches were dragged into the open.

Choi was summoned once more, but this time not in chains. No longer branded a criminal, she was called as a witness. With a trembling voice, she recounted how the accident had begun. She had refused to be forced into selling opium, fearing the new laws that loomed over them. In the struggle, an oil lamp was knocked over, flames consuming everything in moments.

The prince listened, his face stern yet unwavering. When her words were done, he declared her innocent before all present. The brothel was shuttered, its Chinese owner dragged before the crowd and publicly punished. What had begun as a sordid scandal transformed into a victory against a greater evil, a step toward purging corruption from the city's heart.

"I want to thank you so much, Thien," Cheua said, pressing his palms together. "You saved my sister. Without you, we'd be ruined."

"Don't 'wai' me, brother Cheua. That'll shorten my life."

"I judged you wrongly. I thought you were just another flatterer. But now… if you ever need your costume repaired, say the word. I'll make you outshine everyone on stage." Cheua's voice softened, eyes downcast. "I listened to the wrong people." The shame was plain on his face.

Before Thien could say a word, Yod burst into the dormitory, panting and wild-eyed.

"Thien! Sadet Chaokhana wants to see you. Hurry!" Thien followed his friend up the wooden stairs of the golden pavilion, pausing to push open one side of the wide double doors, just enough to step past the threshold. He scanned the main hall, expecting to find Prince Khun Luang seated there, only to glance about in growing unease when no figure appeared.

Catching Yod's eye, he raised his brow in silent question. He had never set foot inside this royal residence before.

"In the library," Yod said briskly. "Go on in. I've got to run." Without waiting for a reply, Cheua dashed off like the wind, his usual laziness forgotten now that dance class awaited.

Thien moved slowly across the veranda to the library on

the left. Its carved door was already ajar, as if waiting for him. At the doorway, he caught sight of the prince within and bowed low, unsure if he had been summoned for praise or reprimand. Prince Khun Luang's expression, when unreadable, often led even the boldest to tread carefully.

"I stopped by your classroom earlier," the prince observed, stepping out to meet him. "Master Maan said you were busy copying a play script. Can you read and write?"

There was a quiet sparkle in his eyes, a sign that this was no interrogation.

"I can, Your Highness," Thien answered respectfully.

"Do you know how to compose verse?"

"I can manage some basic meter."

The prince did not seem surprised. Anyone literate was often taught to compose poetry alongside their lessons.

"Then let's compose one together, shall we?"

"Yes, Your Highness." Thien nodded and sat, back straight, still unsure of the prince's mood until Sadet Chaokhana began the verse himself:

"The clappers sound with echoes pure and deep,"

Thien paused only briefly, then answered…

"In graceful form, the Khon ascends in flight,"

"Old tales unfold as dancers sweep and leap,"

Thien responded, swifter now, the rhythm catching…

"Their movements blaze beneath the golden light."

A faint smile curved the prince's lips, his satisfaction clear.

"Well done. Aside from Master Maan, no one has matched me like this in verse."

"Thank you, Your Highness," Thien replied, heart steadying. He hoped his skill would not make the prince suspect anything, though many men in the capital could read and write. Surely the prince would assume he had studied under KhunPhraNai.

The prince turned back into the royal library and opened a drawer from a tall, Chinese-carved cabinet, its height reaching his waist. He took out an enameled golden pectoral pendant shaped like a lotus bloom, carefully inspecting it to ensure it was the correct one, before stepping out and presenting it to Thien along with a silver box for safekeeping.

"The reward I promised you."

Thien raised both hands above his head to receive the gift. But the moment he laid eyes on the real gold ornament, gleaming brightly in his palm, his mouth dropped open. He had never imagined the prince would bestow something so valuable. He almost wanted to ask whether he truly deserved it.

His adoptive mother had polished gold ornaments in front of him many times, so Thien had learned to distinguish between old and new gold. But this pendant was no ordinary piece. The floral crest rose in exquisite detail, unlike anything he had seen. It was clearly a work of extraordinary craftsmanship that must have taken a long time to complete.

Since the fall of Ayutthaya, the former capital, skilled artisans capable of crafting jewelry of this caliber had become rare. Even the pieces produced by palace goldsmiths could not match the elegance of the pendant now in his hand.

"From now on, after your classes, come here to copy documents. When it's time to rest, go rest. Don't work so late that you miss lessons, understand?" the prince said, not seeming to care whether Thien recognized the pendant's value.

"Yes, Your Highness," Thien replied, bowing low, his forehead touching the polished teak floor.

'Make yourself trustworthy in the master's eyes, but never too conspicuous.' The words of KhunPhraNai echoed in his mind. He knew he had just taken one step closer to gaining the prince's trust.

***

Thien had just stepped off the last teak stair, still lost in awe of the fine lotus crest, when a sudden force jerked him sideways.

Busaba stormed in and snatched the pendant from his hand before Thien even realized he was there.

"You stole it, didn't you? You ungrateful rat!" he hissed, loud enough for heads to turn. "Only the palace smiths can craft this. How dare you sneak into Ruen Horton?"

Thien froze, one foot still on the stair, too stunned to speak. A few dancers nearby stopped in their tracks. The pendant now dangled from Busaba's grip like damning proof in a trial.

"Well, maybe it really was made by the royal goldsmiths, like you said, Busaba, because Sadet Chaokhana gave it to him with his own hand," Yod leaned in, answering everyone's doubt.

"And how would you know that?" someone asked suspiciously.

"Because Sadet Chaokhana told me to fetch him. If not for that, how would Thien have dared see him alone? He doesn't go climbing Sadet Chaokhana's stairs without permission, unlike some people," Yod replied, his voice steady. He had never talked back to Busaba before, but today he did. Perhaps he'd had enough of Busaba's antics.

"So then, it's not stolen. Hand it over," Cheua said as he stepped forward and gripped Busaba's wrist. Being much taller and stronger, he pulled the pendant from the accuser's grasp easily.

"Keep it safe. Don't let anyone retake it. Jealous folks around here aren't in short supply," he added, giving it back to Thien.

The whole troupe fell silent. What was meant to shame Thien had backfired completely. It was Busaba who ended up storming off to his room, slamming the door behind him.

"You're Sadet Chaokhana's favorite now," Yod whispered, nudging Thien with his elbow.

"What does that mean?" Thien asked. Not only curious but wanting to know how he was expected to behave.

"It means you'll be called to perform more often, get more rewards, and have the upper hand over the others." The last part, Yod said louder, making sure the person gnashing her teeth behind the door could hear every word.

***

Yod was right. Being the prince's favorite was not only a mark of honor, it was a golden key. In an age when performances inside the Grand Palace were strictly forbidden and court dancers had become scarce, noble households and city officials turned to troupes outside the palace walls. Increasingly, the Khon ensemble under Prince Khun Luang's patronage was summoned to perform at a wide range of ceremonies. These ranged from topknot-cutting rites for noble children to funerals of high-ranking officials and general blessing rituals.

There were two main types of shows: the curtained stage,

which featured elaborate productions with full sets and scenery that earned the highest fees, and the open hall, performed in the main reception areas of traditional teak houses, with no backdrop, less pomp, but still respected.

The only type of performance Master Maan refused outright was the hired show, the kind staged in front of gambling dens or brothels. He would never allow royal verses, written by the hand of the late king himself, to be sullied by vulgar surroundings.

Now that Thien had begun taking part in outside performances with increasing frequency, he also started receiving greater rewards, such as trinkets of silver, gold bangles, and even the occasional gemstone ring. That was the real power of being the favorite.

In one afternoon, after the music drills and choreography rehearsals had ended, Master Maan gathered the troupe for an important announcement. The prince had personally requested dancers to perform before a visiting Chao Phraya, the provincial lord. It was a prestigious occasion, one every performer aspired to join.

When Master Maan announced the names, Busaba's was called first, followed by Thien's. But before the applause could even begin, Busaba's voice cut through the room like a blade.

"There cannot be two Busabas." She had spoken out against Master Maan before. He usually ignored him, but not today.

"Sadet Chaokhana specifically requested both of you."

"I've never needed a partner to shine. If Master wants to let the new boy gain experience, then I'll graciously step aside."

Gasps rippled through the group. This was a performance for the city's governor himself, and everyone wanted a share of the spotlight. Now Busaba had drawn a line: if Thien went, he would not.

Master Maan exhaled quietly before replying.

"If you do not wish to perform, I won't force you. As I said, the order came from above. I'm not in a position to pick and choose. Unless someone volunteers to forfeit, both names will stand."

His words brought silence over the troupe. No one spoke. No one dared. All except Busaba, who stood fuming. He had been so sure the Master would cast aside his shadow, the other Busaba, and restore the role to him. When it did not happen, his fury boiled over.

It became an unspoken law from that day forward. If Busaba number one took the stage, Thien would not. If Thien performed, Busaba number one would withdraw. There could only ever be one Busaba in the spotlight, just as he had declared.

In the past, when nobles from the provinces came to witness court performances, each palace would host night-long festivities, with grand theatrical displays spanning several days. But now, even a high-ranking Chao Phraya must settle for discreet shows held outside palace grounds. The political climate had changed; lavish entertainment was no longer a safe indulgence.

That evening's performance drew many royal spectators, though most quietly excused themselves after a few hours, fearing that lingering too long might earn the disapproval of His Majesty the king. Only the visiting provincial lord remained in his seat, watching with unwavering interest until the final curtain fell.

When the performers stepped forward to pay respect, one

by one, his eyes halted on Thien.

"Is this the new Busaba?" he asked aloud, his gaze fixed upon the young dancer with undisguised admiration.

"His name is Thien, my lord," said Master Maan, motioning for the boy to crawl closer.

"Such a graceful dancer, with an almost celestial face. Khun Luang, may I request this one be placed in my service?" The lord studied Thien with quiet fascination, his eyes lingering on every movement. He reached out and clasped Thien's hand. Almost without thinking, Thien pulled his hand back.

The boy's heart plummeted, panic surging through him. His eyes darted toward the prince, tears burning at the corners. He longed to refuse, but etiquette bound his tongue. All his carefully laid plans might unravel with this single request.

The prince saw it and understood. He stepped forward with composure, his voice steady and calm.

"He is still inexperienced. I fear that sending him would only invite embarrassment. There are other dancers far more suited."

Everyone present knew the prince's word was final. The

lord gave a soft sigh.

"What a pity. I had heard you had two Busabas."

The prince offered no reply. Realizing he would not win this prize, the lord reached into his robes and pulled out a gold ring, placing it in Thien's hand.

"Should you ever wish to visit my provinces, you need only ask."

He clasped Thien's hand tightly, reluctant to let go as though holding a rare treasure. This time, Thien didn't pull away. To do so again might offend. After a moment, the lord finally released him.

Thien retreated to the end of the line as the next performer stepped forward. When the room filled with cheerful chatter, he slipped away, the weight of his costume and the heavy jewelry pressing down on him. He longed for air and peace.

Standing beneath the ylang-ylang tree, he let the breeze cool his skin until a familiar voice spoke behind him.

"Why didn't you go with Chao Phraya?"

Thien startled, then dropped to his knees, bowing low.

"Your Highness …" He hesitated, then asked what had been gnawing at his heart. "Does the lord often ask to take performers into his service?"

"Quite often," the prince replied. "Some become dance masters, others his household's entertainers. Some personal attendants. If lucky… a consort."

"A consort?" Thien's voice rose in surprise.

"Beautiful dancers are sometimes taken as wives or concubines. If fate favors them, perhaps even as royal consorts."

Thien swallowed hard.

"I am content to serve under Your Highness," he said quietly. "And… I'm not even sure what role the lord had in mind for me. As you said, I am not yet very skilled."

"You're sulking because I said you're not yet skilled?" the prince raised an eyebrow.

"No, Your Highness. I understood your words were a gentle refusal for my sake. I am grateful for your protection, and I wish to remain in your service always."

The prince gave a thoughtful nod.

"What day, month, and year were you born?"

Thien tensed. The royal astrologer had warned him never to disclose this, especially not to the prince. The prince was rumored to be gifted in astrology, even being praised by the late king.

"I don't know, Your Highness. I was orphaned at birth. KhunPraNai took me in, then sent me here when he saw I loved poetry and dance."

The prince acknowledged with a slight nod, then turned wordlessly back to the hall.

Chapter 3

Lately, Prince Khun Luang had been spending nearly every night at Ruen Horton, always accompanied by stacks of documents to work through. As a result, Thien had seldom found the chance to go out or spend time with friends—until now. The prince had sent word of his journey to Ayutthaya, a message that reached Thien with the news he would not be returning. Seizing the rare opportunity, Thien eagerly joined Muang and Chuea for a stroll through the Tha-Phra Palace market, a bustling bazaar just behind the grand palace walls.

"Can I invite Yot along too?" Thien asked, knowing full well Yot's feelings for Muang. Leaving him out might cost their friendship.

"Don't worry about Yot. He's already waiting on the

boat," Chuea said, pointing toward the river landing. They were clearly waiting for him before setting off.

Tha-Phra Palace was once the residence of the eldest son of the previous monarch before he ascended the throne as King Rama III. At the rear of the palace, a bustling market thrived, offering a variety of goods both on boats and on land.

Thien had never set foot there before, and the sight of Thai and Chinese merchants lining the area with their wares left him utterly dazzled. Among the many stalls, the one Chuea led them to stood out the most. He introduced the betel seller as his half-sister, the very woman Thien had once helped.

"This is my friend Thien. He's the one who helped you back then," Chuea said.

At the mention of his name, Choi's eyes widened. She stepped from behind her stall and bowed deeply, so much so that Thien barely had time to return the gesture.

The two siblings, born to a nobleman, were humble and kind. Though Thien had few friends and rarely spoke unless he felt at ease, those like Yot and Chuea had always watched over him, teaching him, guiding him, and helping him see more of the world.

Then, without warning, the thought struck him. A pang of guilt weighed on his chest. He was still keeping his true identity hidden from the troupe.

After the trial, Sister Choi did not return to our father's household. She chose instead to live with Thit Mak and has since helped him tend this humble stall.

Thit Mak had once been a frequent visitor to the Green Lantern brothel. Yet he never once scorned Choi for her past life. Even while she was imprisoned, he sent her food and supplies without fail. Choi was touched by his quiet devotion and agreed to marry him. Thit Mak wasn't much to look at, but he was kind and steady. Choi, on the other hand, was beautiful and radiant, like that of a royal consort; her face now shone with quiet joy, free at last from the weight of suffering.

"Please, take this. A little something to show my gratitude," Choi said before Thien could leave, handing him a complete set of betel wrapped in fresh leaves.

"You should sell it instead. I've never chewed betel before. I wouldn't know how." He waved his hand in refusal.

"Nonsense. I'll roll it for you," Choi replied, her hands moving with practiced ease. Back in her brothel days, she'd done it often for patrons, and her fingers worked with grace and speed.

"Thien's still a kid, Choi. Look at those teeth. White like a pup's," Chuea teased. Others in the troupe had tried to get Thien to chew before, but he always pulled a face and refused after the first bite, complaining it was too spicy.

"This is Chinese betel leaf. Not as spicy as the green kind. Here." She handed it to him.

Thien, out of politeness, took the roll and placed it in his mouth. But after only two chews, he spat out the pulp.

"It's still spicy!"

"Can I try?" Muang asked sweetly.

But before she could reach for it, Yot swooped in and popped the chewed betel into his own mouth.

"No way. I'm eating it. If you two share this, people will think you're romantically involved," Yot said. He didn't want Muang tasting Thien's betel. That was a bad omen. According to old beliefs, sharing betel meant deepening a bond. He didn't want to fight his best friend over the same girl.

"Yot, you bastard! Spit it out! I don't want to share anything with you either!" Thien snapped, trying to pry Yot's mouth open, but the thief dashed away.

"Wow, Choi's betel really is delicious. Just the right kick," Yot praised, mouth stained with crimson juice.

Choi and Chuea burst out laughing at the two friends' bickering, but a voice from a nearby stall broke the moment.

"Isn't that the Khon actor from Prince Khun Luang's troupe?"

Thien turned toward the speaker. A dark-skinned man with a scraggly mustache, clearly unshaven and unpleasant. At first, Thien thought he might be a fan. But the sneer on the man's face and the derisive glance he cast, especially at Thien, made it clear otherwise.

"Let's go," Chuea urged. The man's companions were all burly men. Without hesitation, Chuea bade his sister goodbye and quickly led the younger ones away before trouble could begin.

Thien furrowed his brows in confusion but said nothing. He couldn't understand why the man looked at him with such disdain.

***

Thien ended up taking the bundle of betel back to the troupe, intending to share it with Sadet Chaokhana. If the prince knew it was from Choi, he would surely be pleased.

"Hearing Choi's story gave me hope," Yot whispered to Thien as they trailed behind Chuea and Muang.

"Hope about what?"

"Muang, of course! If someone as beautiful as Choi could fall for a plain guy like Thit Mak, I stand a chance. I'm way better looking than that guy."

Yot had a point. He was indeed a handsome fellow. Even Master Maan once said that if Yot danced better, he could've been cast as a heroic lead.

That night, after returning and having dinner at the troupe house, Thien went to store the betel bundle in the drawer by his bed. But when he opened it, he discovered that the silver box containing the royal pendant was gone!

"Yot! The pendant that Sadet Chaokhana gave me!!! It's gone!"

Thien opened each drawer, pulling everything out one by one and placing it aside. He spent a long time searching. The room wasn't big. Each person had their own glass cabinet at the end of the bed. However, even after reviewing all of them, there was no sign of the box.

"Did you lend it to someone? Did you check your fabric pouch?" Yot mumbled sleepily. He had taken a bath and gone to bed earlier than the rest, and when shaken awake with the news, he only poked his head out from under the blanket before drifting back to sleep.

Thien went to check the cloth pouch he had used when he first arrived at the troupe, but the pendant wasn't there either. He didn't want to wake Yot again, so he lay back in bed, staring at the ceiling with a heavy heart, wondering how he'd ever find the thief if someone really had stolen it.

***

Despite Prince Khun Luang himself stating that he did not want Thian to work late into the night, the moment he returned from the old city, he unloaded a mountain of documents onto Thian's desk, demanding they be copied in full. Even though it was nearly midnight, he still wouldn't let Thian rest, continuing to order him to correct his work.

"Thian, what has come over you today? Your writing is careless and untidy. If you submit your work in this state, I shall have no choice but to correct it myself. Do you understand?" Prince Khun Luang's furious words cut through the chamber like a blade. His voice was not one of disdain, but rather a mark of familiarity —a tone reserved only for those closest to him. Months of working together had granted Thian a level of informality that others could only dream of.

"I beg Your Highness's forgiveness. I was careless and failed to proofread properly…" Thian hurriedly bowed his head so low it nearly touched the floor.

But his mind was elsewhere, entangled in a dilemma. Should he confess to Prince Khun Luang that the royal pendant he had been granted had been stolen? If he kept silent, the culprit might never be caught. But if he spoke, the prince might suspect he had sold it himself. This torment clouded Thian's mind, affecting his work and leading to more mistakes, which earned him more reprimands.

Prince Khun Luang studied Thian closely, his gaze unreadable. But before he could speak, the entire house shuddered violently. Walls creaked. Floorboards groaned. As if shaken by a powerful force from deep beneath or all around.

Then came the sound. Faint at first, like something pulled from memory, then rising and trumpeting cries of elephants, followed by the pounding roar of heavy feet thundering past in a frenzied stampede.

Thian stood frozen, breath caught in his chest. Elephants? Here? That was impossible. They were in the heart of the capital, surrounded by bustling streets, imposing buildings, and formidable walls. No such creatures could roam free without causing alarm.

He turned to the prince, ready to ask if he had heard it too, but the prince spoke first, his tone sharp and urgent.

"Do you still have the pectoral pendant?"

The question struck like a bolt of lightning. Thian's blood turned to ice. His lips parted, but the words caught in his throat.

"May Your Highness's judgment be merciful. I can no longer find it," Thian confessed, voice unsteady. "Yesterday, I went to the market near the palace. When I returned… it was gone."

Now it wasn't just the teakwood house that trembled. Thian was shaking just as hard. He had committed not one, but two offenses: the careless transcription and now the loss of a royal gift. And yet… how? How did Prince Khun Luang already know the pendant was missing?

He didn't have long to wonder. The tremor faded, but a new disturbance broke the quiet, shouts and hurried footsteps from the sleeping quarters of the Khon performers.

Then came a scream.

"Aaahhh!!" A terrified cry, unmistakably Busaba's, rang through the halls, chilling Thian to the bone. Instinctively, he shot to his feet, ready to run and see what had happened.

But the prince raised a hand, halting him where he was.

"There's no need to go," the prince said calmly. "Remain here and finish transcribing the records. As for the missing item, if it was ever truly yours, it will find its way back."

Thian hesitated, confusion tightening in his chest. "Your Highness… what do you mean?" he asked, tilting his head, hands still joined in apology.

Though fear of the prince's wrath lingered, months of working side by side had stripped away

"All things," the prince replied, his voice low and deliberate, "belong to someone by fate. Even if lost or stolen, they are returned to their rightful owner in a timely manner. That pendant. It's no mere ornament. It's ancient, passed down through generations. Only those of true fortune are meant to possess it. If it's gone, let it be. If it is yours, it will return. But if it is not… keeping it would only bring ruin upon you and your bloodline."

He spoke no more.

The house, which only moments earlier had groaned under invisible weight, now stood utterly still. The phantom cries of elephants faded into silence. Even Busaba's scream had vanished like a ripple lost to calm waters.

***

Three days passed, and Thien still hadn't discovered who stole the pendant. Meanwhile, Busaba had not returned to rehearse since the strange incident with the elephants that night.

Master Maan reported that Busaba had fallen gravely ill,

confirmed by Yod's whispered warning that he had seen a ghost. Even Yod's claim seemed unbelievable to everyone else until he insisted.

Only Master Maan was permitted to visit Busaba. He quietly separated those who shared rooms with him, citing quarantine, and had Muang deliver three daily meals to Busaba's door. Each time, only her hand would emerge to receive the food before he vanished again behind the closed door.

Thian still couldn't shake his doubt about the elephant sounds that night. Everyone insisted that Master Mann kept no elephants, but the memory lingered.

"Do you really want to see an elephant, brother Thien? Why do you keep asking about it?" Muang tugged at her sleeve and whispered beside the kitchen.

"If there is one, then yes, I'd like to see it."

It was strange. No one else had heard the sound that night, so he couldn't be sure if it were real or just his imagination.

"There is one! And if you truly want to see it, I'll take you. But you mustn't bring anyone else," Muang said, her expression suddenly serious, not her usual cheeky self.

So Thian agreed to go with her alone, as she asked, and they settled on a time.

She guided Thien behind the theater garden, along an old, seldom-used path that led toward a river wharf. Instead of crossing the wooden bridge, she dodged through a banana-leaf screen, emerging into fields with a small shed where laborers rested.

"This is our secret spot. Promise me you won't tell Yod," she warned, her gaze sweeping over the verdant paddy.

"Where's the elephant?" Thien asked, scanning the landscape.

"Be patient. Wait till the sun begins to fall, the mahout will bring the bull out to drink right over there." She pointed to the far edge of the field.

Thien sat quietly, waiting. Then Muang spoke softly.

"Brother, may I ask you something?"

Muang turned to look at him, her hair tied in a topknot, her face delicate and slender, with wide, clear eyes full of innocence. Now that they had grown closer, Thian had come to see her as a younger sister, not as the girl who once harbored a quiet affection for him. It made it easier for him to speak with her without reserve.

"Yes."

"Are you… one of those who prefer men?"

Thian frowned at her bluntness.

"Why do you ask?"

"I just want to know if I ever had a chance," she said, utterly unashamed. He flicked her forehead with a sigh.

"You cheeky child."

"Ow!" she laughed, rubbing the spot with a grin.

"Where's the elephant, then? If there's none, I'm going back to Ruen Horton," Thian said, beginning to rise.

"It's all right if you don't like me. I like you because you dance so beautifully. I wish I could dance like you and Busaba," Muang said. She sprang to her feet and started mimicking Busaba's Siang Thian pose, the Khon dance that Master Maan had once demonstrated. But her hands were stiff, and her steps wobbled. She had never learned the basic postures properly.

"If you want to learn, why not ask Master Maan to teach

you?"

"He won't let me. He said it's not a proper profession for a girl. But I don't want to perform for anyone. I want to dress up beautifully and dance to the music," Muang replied, shaping her hands and arms into a crude pose as she spoke.

Then suddenly, her eyes widened in surprise. She pointed toward the edge of the field.

"There! Look! An elephant comes out to drink!" Sure enough, just as Muang had said, the mahout led the elephant out to drink from the ridge of the field. But there was only one elephant, not a whole herd.

Muang beamed with pride, relieved not to be accused of lying.

They watched the elephant in silence for a while before Thian finally spoke.

"If you really want to learn, I'll teach you. Consider it a reward for bringing me to see the elephant."

"Really?" Her eyes sparkled with delight.

"We can practice here. I come and sit here every day. No

one ever passes this way."

Her smile stretched nearly ear to ear, and it made Thian smile, too.

***

Thien ran, breath catching in his throat, weaving through the banana grove behind the garden. He'd lost track of time chatting with Muan. By the time he realized, the sun was already sinking low. The path across the field, once short and familiar, now stretched endlessly. No matter how fast he ran, the Ruen Horton never seemed to get any closer.

"Oi, Thien! Where've you been all day?" Yot called out, waving a banana leaf bundle in the air. "Sadet Chaokhana brought desserts from the palace!"

"Can't! I am late!" Thien shouted back without slowing.

He dashed to the dragon-etched water jar, dipped out a scoop with a coconut ladle, and rinsed the dirt from his feet. Gasping for breath, he tiptoed up the steps, praying the prince hadn't yet noticed he was gone.

But something was odd. As soon as he crossed the threshold, he heard a voice singing from inside the bedchamber, a room whose doors were usually shut tight but now stood slightly ajar.

Curious as to which guest would be allowed into the prince's private quarters, Thien crept forward on his knees. He had no wish to eavesdrop, only to ask whether he should wait or return to his quarters later.

Candlelight flickered brightly inside, casting clear shadows on the occupants within.

There, seated at the foot of the bed, was the prince himself, dressed in nothing but a loosely tied lower cloth. He had clearly been home for some time, as he often shed his upper garments when not attending court. And before him danced Busaba, her voice reciting verse, his arms weaving graceful motions as he performed a new choreography supposedly developed with the master teacher.

Though he wore a formal chong kraben and a tall crown, his upper body was bare, exposed in the same way as the prince's own. Thien stiffened. His face flushed hot. He intended to retreat, but his eyes wouldn't look away.

The prince rose and extended his hand to Busaba, taking

his hand into a paired posture like those in Khon dramas. Busaba pressed gently against his chest, their movements in sync, as if from a painted scene in a romance poem.

Thien felt his chest tighten, not with anger, but with something unnameable envy. Especially when the prince corrected Busaba's pose with a soft touch. He hadn't known Sadet Chaokhana could dance Khon.

Their lesson didn't last long. However, it had begun as a simple demonstration of a newly choreographed dance. The air inside the room soon thickened, heavy with an unspoken tension that crackled like a storm held just beneath the surface.

Candlelight flickered against the polished floor, casting gold and amber shadows across the silk-draped room. The prince stood tall, bare-chested, every movement elegant yet quietly powerful. Busaba moved in rhythm, his gestures fluid but deliberate, each motion drawing him nearer to the prince. Sweat beaded on his brow, not just from exertion but from something more volatile—desire coiled beneath his skin.

Then Busaba lifted his hand and placed it gently upon the prince's chest. His touch lingered. His fingers splayed across the warm skin, and for a heartbeat, neither of them moved. The prince's gaze didn't waver, but a new gleam surfaced within it, one of recognition and permission.

Busaba's lips curled upward with delight. The prince grasped Busaba's hand, firm, commanding, yet not unkind. With his other hand, he reached for the ornate golden belt at his waist. A soft clink sounded as the clasp came undone.

The long silken wrap slid down his hips in a slow cascade, pooling at his feet like water spilled from a gilded bowl. The prince stepped forward, not as royalty, not as a teacher or sovereign, but as a man moved by an emotion he could no longer resist. The prince pulled Busaba into his arms. In that still moment, all the walls between them crumbled.

Thien's entire body tensed. His breath caught as Busaba lay back upon the bed, inviting. The prince followed, his well-toned form moving with ease as he leaned over the dancer. Startled, Thien flinched and knocked the door open further.

The prince turned at once, eyes narrowed. Yet he saw no one in the hallway. His brow furrowed for a moment, but relaxed again when Busaba whispered,

"What was that noise, Your Highness?"

"Probably just the cat," he said, though he knew very well it was not. The cat never wandered the house when guests were present.

***

Thien wept on the way back to his dormitory. Thankfully, Yot and Boonmak were still in the kitchen, distracted by the sweet desserts from the palace. No one saw him wipe his tears with the hem of his cloth.

Why was he crying for an enemy?

Shock. Betrayal. Jealousy. Was it the pain of seeing the prince with someone else? Or had he deluded himself into thinking he was the only favored one, just because he served the prince each night?

Both Busaba and Prince Khun Luang were his enemies. One had tried to drive him from the Khon troupe. The other had condemned his father to die in prison.

Thien pounded his fist into his pillow. The images tormented him. Busaba's hands on the prince, the intimacy in their dance, the kind that could only come from many nights

Khon Spy Behind the Fallen Prince

before this one.

He had been by the prince's side every night. Even the household cat, who avoided everyone else, came to sit beside him during long hours in the script room. Yet the prince had never once looked at him like that.

Busaba remained the chosen one—the first and only favorite.

***

In the Kudeejeen neighborhood stood a Chinese apothecary open late into the night. The old man inside spoke only Mandarin, but he understood Thai well enough.

When Thien asked for something to help him sleep, the man went to his drawers and pulled out three dried herbs, including chrysanthemum flowers and jujube seeds.

"How much?" Thien asked, though in truth, he had no trouble sleeping.

The old man waved him off and gestured for him to leave.

Thien hadn't walked far from the shop when he sensed someone following him. But each time he turned, no one was there.

It wasn't until he reached the drama hall that he spotted Master Maan and KhunPhraNai sitting together at the kitchen bench.

Thien rubbed his eyes, hardly believing what he saw. How had the man arrived so quickly? If he were cast in a Khon play, surely he'd play Hanuman, the monkey god.

"There you are, Thien. You have a guest," the old master called, gesturing him over.

Thien bowed deeply to both men and said nothing until Master Maan excused himself.

"I'll go bathe. Please, make yourself at home, sir."

Now alone with his unexpected visitor, Thien knew this was not a conversation they could have in public. He led the man past the banana trees behind the kitchen to a secluded spot Muang had once shown him.

She'd sworn him to secrecy about this place, but KhunPhraNai wasn't Yot. Thien exhaled, only half guilty for breaking his word.

"How did you come to know this place?" KhunPhraNai asked, his lantern casting a flickering glow beneath the waxing moon.

"Muan, Master Maan's niece, told me," he said plainly, knowing the details weren't what the lord had come for. He glanced around to be sure no one would overhear.

"I hear you've become a favorite," the man said. "Congratulations."

"That matter…" Thien sighed. With the scent of rain on the wind, he skipped the pleasantries and got straight to the point.

"May I be reassigned? I'm willing to serve in any other capacity but this work…"

"Where is that bold young man who volunteered to avenge his father?" KhunPhraNai's voice grew sharp, though Thien couldn't tell if the redness in his face came from the lantern or disappointment.

"I truly can't continue this task," he admitted, ashamed that he'd let his emotions show. How could he face the prince now?

"I still wish to avenge my father. But if I remain, I will be exposed sooner or later. I don't want anyone to suffer because of my failure."

He hadn't expected to run from the Ruen Horton in tears. If anyone had stopped him then, he might've told them everything.

"No one has reported you yet. What are you afraid of?"

"Reported?" Thien's brows furrowed.

"You think there's only one spy in the troupe?" the nobleman asked knowingly.

"The Prince's circle has ears everywhere like pineapples," he added dryly. "If they can't plant their own among enemies, they'll simply buy them. Just keep studying. Stay close to Sadet Chakhana as you've been doing. You won't be exposed." He clapped Thien's shoulder. It wasn't forceful, but the sheer size of his hand nearly sent the smaller man stumbling.

"Who is the other spy in the troupe?" Thien asked. "One day, you'll know. For now, I can't tell you. Just remember. If I sense you're in danger, I'll get you out. Look, you needed me tonight, and here I am."

Thien nodded. He still wasn't sure he'd succeed, but at least the pressure had eased. "Never forget, the prince is the one who had your father imprisoned. As long as he holds power, the common folk will live in fear, for there is no justice left in the courts."

Even though Thien hadn't yet found proof that Prince Khun Luang took bribes, he remained certain of one truth: his father had been a good man—a good man who should not have died behind bars.

And that was enough reason to continue.

Chapter 4

Every Thursday, the khon troupe finished practice early. The day began with a morning sacred performance to pay respect to their masters, as incense smoke drifted through the air and the sound of ancient rhythms rang out under the open pavilion. Afterward, they could spend the rest of the day as they wished. Some wandered off to the market, others lingered in the garden or caught up on sleep in the shade.

Thien was wrapping a fresh indigo cloth around his hips, already planning to drag Yot and Chuea out for grilled pork skewers and iced sugarcane juice, when a knock came—sharp and rushed.

"Thien! Sadet Chaokhana wants you!" Yot's voice rang through the door, breathless with urgency.

"What!?" Thien nearly tripped over his own feet. "Why?"

This wasn't his duty day. He had no errands, no assignments at the Ruen Horton. There was no reason to be summoned.

Unless…A voice in his head, petty and uninvited, chimed in.

Why not call Busaba instead? That peacock would prance there in a heartbeat if it meant getting one toe closer to the prince.

Still muttering curses under his breath, Thien tied his cloth tighter and stepped into the corridor. Just as he passed the kitchen, a familiar scent of jasmine and rose oil wafted past—Busaba, gliding by like a silk fan, gave him a sideways glance and a sharp flick of the hip.

Thien didn't bite. He kept his eyes ahead, slowed his pace, and tried to appear utterly disinterested.

He wasn't eager to arrive. In truth, his stomach was twisted in knots.

Should I apologize for last night? Or pretend nothing happened?

He chose silence.

Let Sadet Chaokhana be the one to bring it up. If he even cared to mention it at all.

When he reached the hall, he saw the prince standing by the dais, waiting. Thien bowed low in a full prostration, keeping his head down and bracing for reprimand. He didn't notice that the prince's eyes were softer than usual.

"You came all the way here and didn't call for me. Why?"

The tone was gentle, but the message left no room for doubt. The prince knew it had been Thien outside his chamber the night before.

"I didn't mean to disturb Your Highness," Thien replied barely above a whisper, both arms resting in a respectful posture before him. His gaze remained fixed on the floor.

There was a moment of stillness, as though the air itself held its breath.

"Then why do you sound upset, hmm?" the prince asked. His voice carried a playful lilt, but the edge beneath it was unmistakable.

"I wouldn't dare, Your Highness," Thien turned his head slightly, avoiding the prince's eyes.

"Your words and your face are telling me different things."

Thien stayed silent, his expression unreadable.

"So tell me. What's troubling you?"

"Please, Your Highness… don't concern yourself with the petty feelings of someone like me."

Still, Thien did not explain. He stood frozen, lips pressed together.

The prince studied him for a moment longer before asking what he truly wished to know.

"Last night… what did you see?"

He sat down on the raised dais, gazing down at Thien to reassert his authority.

"Nothing, Your Highness," Thien answered quickly, feeling like a criminal awaiting judgment.

"Liar. If you saw something, say so. No need to pretend."

"I only saw how graceful Your Highness danced. I never imagined you could perform khon so well…"

Thien's cheeks flushed at the memory of how close the two bodies had moved together.

"If I couldn't dance, how could I be the patron of the royal khon troupe?"

"There are plenty of lords who keep troupes just for the sake of status," Thien answered, his tone edged with frankness.

The prince gave a low chuckle.

"There you are—that sharp-tongued Thien who always twists my words and bites back with logic. I was beginning to wonder if you'd lost your voice altogether."

He reached behind and retrieved a shiny silver box.

"Come closer."

Thien crept closer, puzzled as the prince extended the box to him. He took it with a bow, not knowing what to expect. But when he opened it, he gasped.

Thien obeyed, stepping forward with cautious eyes. The prince extended the box toward him, and Thien received it with a bow, unsure of what lay within. The weight in his hands felt oddly familiar.

He lifted the lid. A sharp breath escaped his lips. There, nestled on a bed of dark velvet, was the missing royal pendant.

"How did you find this, Your Highness?" he whispered, eyes wide with disbelief.

"That's not your concern," the prince replied smoothly. "Didn't I tell you? If something truly belongs to someone, it will find its way back. But if it doesn't, it'll vanish again."

Thien bowed deeply at his feet; all hesitation about facing the prince was now melted away. A smile broke across his face without effort.

"Did Your Highness summon me just for this? Or shall I assist with your correspondence, too?"

Even though it was his day off, Thien was eager to stay and serve. Going to the market no longer interested him.

"You wanted to know if I could dance, didn't you? Then get up and match rhythms with me. Let's see which of us is the better dancer."

"I'll let Your Highness win," Thien teased, grinning with childlike warmth. "You're gifted in every art, like Ravana himself, with ten heads and twenty arms. There's nothing you can't do."

"So now you're not so sharp-tongued, eh?"

"If Your Highness says I talk too much, does that mean I've got the mouth of a mongrel?" Thien laughed nervously and bowed again, hands raised above his head in full surrender.

***

That night, Thien dreamed of elephants gathered in a vast, mist-veiled field under an evening sky, standing like sentinels of a forgotten world. He didn't know where he was. The land held no people, no borders, no hint of home, yet it called to him with a strange familiarity. A tusker of immense size, larger than the rest, stepped forward. Its eyes are dark and ancient. It bent its head low, as though inviting Thien to climb onto its back.

He froze. He had never ridden an elephant before. The height alone was daunting. But as he looked into the creature's eyes, a strange trust took hold. Without knowing why, he reached up and pulled himself onto its broad back.

Against his chest, the royal pectoral pendant grazed his skin. The sensation jolted him. This was no ordinary dream.

The great elephant turned, and they began to move slowly through veils of mist that parted to reveal a vision from another time.

Ayutthaya.

Not the ruined, overgrown Ayutthaya of memory, but the Ayutthaya of legend: golden rooftops blazing beneath the sun, temple spires piercing the sky, monks gliding across polished courtyards like ripples on water. The city shimmered with life. It was glorious. Breathtaking in its beauty.

Thien smiled, eyes wide with awe.

Then, from somewhere far away… a rooster crowed.

Thien's eyes snapped open. He startled and looked around. The room was unfamiliar. The ceiling above him was made of teakwood, not plaster, unlike in his own quarters. He turned his head from side to side until he realized he was in the royal scriptorium.

Memories of the night before hit him like a flood: The prince had invited him to drink Namtan Mao, that sweet, potent sugar wine. One cup had sent his head spinning. Drunk and babbling, he'd gone on to suggest they perform a Khon scene together.

He had dared to make the prince play Tosakanth, while he himself played Sita, imprisoned and defiant. He had even recited rude verses at the demon king without a shred of shame.

Oh gods.

Thien slapped his forehead. Would I be executed for insulting royalty in verse? That sugar wine. Never again. One time was enough. It had scrambled his thoughts and left him unable to find his way back to his own quarters. The prince must have carried him here.

Panicked, Thien threw on a fresh wrap and dashed down to the riverfront to wash. Once the cold water had cleared his head, he looked back up at the Ruen Horton. And there stood the prince, watching him calmly from the balcony.

Mortified, Thien turned away immediately, pretending not to see him.

"You're dead, Thien. You're so dead this time. One mess after another. Can't even keep your own mouth shut," he muttered, knocking himself on the head. Then he bolted for his quarters like lightning.

***

Thien's name was starting to gain recognition, rising alongside the growing fame of Prince Khun Luang's Khon troupe. Whenever the troupe was invited to perform outside the palace, the prince would lead them in full ceremonial dress, riding a royal barge down the Chao Phraya River. Villagers along the banks would come out to watch, drawn by the shimmering silk, golden masks, and graceful movements of the dancers.

No one enjoyed the attention more than Busaba. He loved the grandeur. Even on days without a performance, he would stroll through temple fairs dressed like a noblewoman from old Ayutthaya, eager to be seen and admired.

Thien was nothing like Busaba. As soon as the performance ended, he slipped away to the dressing room, unfastening the brocaded cloth and lifting the Khon mask from his face as though discarding a borrowed identity. He never lingered. He kept his gaze low, careful to avoid the stares—and the word that never failed to follow.

Kathoey.

The villagers tossed it around carelessly, using it to describe any man in women's dress. It didn't matter whether he was an artist, a comedian, or a sacred dancer; to them, the label fit all the same. Spoken with a grin or a sneer, it stripped away the dignity behind the costume.

But what wounded deeper than the word itself was the way parents reacted. Mothers would pull their sons close. Fathers would turn their children's heads. They shielded young eyes as if a glance could taint them. As if watching a dancer might inspire imitation—or worse, affection.

No one seemed to remember that Khon had once been a royal art, taught in royal halls with reverence and pride. It carried history, dignity, and the breath of a nation's soul. Now it was little more than a spectacle, and those who kept it alive were treated not as guardians of tradition but as curiosities to be mocked. Even the King had stopped teaching Khon inside the palace. If the ordinary people scorned the art and ridiculed those who kept it alive… who would carry it forward?

Who would remember what it was meant to be?

Khon Spy Behind the Fallen Prince

Not long ago, an anonymous letter had been left at the temple gate, accusing Prince Khun Luang of having an affair with one of his actors and neglecting his royal consorts in the palace.

At first, the prince had fumed like a ten-headed Ravana when courtiers came to report it. But as more came bearing the same whispers, he dismissed them all with a wave of the hand. Today, Thien finally dared to ask:

"Your Highness… aren't you going to investigate who started these rumors?"

"If His Majesty the King sees no cause to pursue it, then neither do I. Those who hide behind letters are cowards. If they truly had the courage, they'd confront me face-to-face."

Thien's spine prickled at those words. He thought of his adoptive father, accused and imprisoned over a similar anonymous letter. One that the prince's men had brought before the throne. In the chaos that followed, many were hunted down for questioning. His father, though innocent, had taken the blame… and died behind bars.

The memory made Thien clench his fists. His vision blurred with tears, and he quickly wiped away before anyone could see.

"I'll be traveling to Ayutthaya for the Loi Krathong festival this twelfth full moon. You're coming with me. Be ready," the prince suddenly said, shifting the conversation to the upcoming event three months away.

"But… why so far, Your Highness? There will be numerous Krathong festivals in the capital. Why make the journey?"

"I want you to meet someone. A respected elder who's long wished to see you."

Thien flinched, his eyes wide with alarm, just like the time a provincial governor had asked whether he wanted to be assigned to the outer cities.

"I'm not sending you away, if that's what you're afraid of," the prince muttered, catching the look on his face.

"Who else is going?" Thien asked, thinking of Busaba, the other favored performer.

"You may bring whomever you like," came the clipped reply. "I've invited no one else but you."

Khon Spy Behind the Fallen Prince

The prince reached for the betel set that Muan's mother always prepared, arranging it neatly on a gilded tray beside a glass of passionfruit juice whenever Sadet Chaokhana arrived. Thien winced at the memory of the sharp, bitter taste he'd once dared to try.

Perhaps he was the only man in the capital who refused to chew betel. But he couldn't stand the taste. He never understood how others managed it.

"Want a taste?" The prince offered him the entire set of betel.

"I'll pass, Your Highness," Thien said, shaking his head quickly.

"Why?"

"It's too spicy."

"Not mine. Mine's sweet."

"Everyone says that, Your Highness. But every time I try, it burns my mouth."

The prince laughed at his honesty.

"You just don't know how to chew it properly, Thien."

"That's exactly why I'd rather not, Your Highness."

"You again, always arguing with me," the prince grumbled with mock irritation. "If I weren't so indulgent, you'd have been whipped for your impertinence by now." But the prince was smiling. Thien recognized the glint in his eye as he clapped his palm loudly on his own knee.

"The first bite is bitter," the prince explained while chewing slowly. "Chew gently. Let your tongue savor the taste, and the sweetness will come." He beckoned Thien closer.

Thien obeyed.

The prince spat out the chewed quid and held it to Thien's lips. Sharing betel this way was a traditional sign of intimacy, as Yot once explained before, "A gesture of affection and trust."

Thien didn't even glance at the prince's fingertips. He opened his mouth, caught in the soft sincerity of that gaze. Couldn't say no.

The prince, so divine, so high above, had come down to share betel with a lowly actor. What lifetime of merit had earned him this?

One hand lifted Thien's chin; the other slipped the betel

gently into his mouth. The first taste numbed his lips. His eyes clenched shut. But then he remembered the prince's words: Chew gently. The sweetness will come.

And it did.

The bitterness faded, replaced by coolness and the herbal scent of the leaf. His heart, too, felt strangely full, as if joy had seeped through his veins. It made that one bite of betel sweeter than any he'd ever imagined.

He opened his eyes and saw the prince's radiant face, so close it seemed divinely lit. His fingers lingered against Thien's chin. Their breaths mingled.

The prince's fingers gently wiped the reddish juice from the corner of Thien's mouth. Then his face leaned even closer. So near that Thien could smell the same spice and warmth of the betel between them.

"So?" the prince whispered. "Do you taste the sweetness now?"

The spell broke. The prince pulled away.

Thien bowed low, pressing his palms together and burying his burning face against the floor.

"A little, Your Highness," he murmured.

He hadn't really chewed the betel. His heart was thudding too hard to think straight. And yet... he felt happy. Strangely happy.

So this was the taste of real betel. Not on the tongue, but in the heart. A sweetness not of flavor, but of feeling.

He wanted to remain there, lying beside the prince's feet forever. To serve him. To adore him. In this life and the next.

***

Busaba had kept his distance from Thien ever since that night's scream, though he still visited the Ruen Horton once a week as usual. On those days when he met with the prince, Thien's duties were quietly set aside. He didn't go up to copy records, and the prince didn't summon him. It was, in effect, a day off for Thien.

The paddy field behind the garden had become a secret classroom for teaching dance to Muan. She had a natural talent and quickly memorized the script and movements. True to the saying that "the apple doesn't fall far from the tree," she was the niece of Master Maan.

On his walk home after teaching Muan, Thien found KhunPhraNai waiting outside the kitchen. He had already been there some time, even though Thien hadn't gone to the apothecary.

KhunPhraNai had sent a signal earlier, instructing him to meet here at midnight at the secret field.

Thien had bathed, changed, and gone to sleep early. Now, under the moonlit paddy, he encountered KhunPhraNai, who stood quietly with a faint smile.

"I hear you're going to the Loy Krathong festival with Sadet Chaokhana," KhunPhraNai said.

"Yes, sir. We depart the day after tomorrow," Thien answered truthfully. The prince had allowed him to bring friends, so he had invited Yot and Chuea. Chuea's family was originally from Ayutthaya. While Yot had never been to the old capital, he was pleased to be invited.

KhunPhraNai closed his eyes as if to savor the moment, then looked back at Thien. "It begins, then," he murmured before continuing: "I want you to ask Sadet Chaokhana to bring another Khon actor along."

"Whom, sir?"

Thien realized this must be the spy KhunPhraNai had mentioned before, the other infiltrator among the troupe. He had asked once but received no answer. Perhaps this mission was important enough for KhunPhraNai to reveal the spy's identity now.

KhunPhraNai didn't reply directly. Instead, he nodded toward a clump of banana trees. Emerging from the shadows was Busaba. Thien nearly fell over in surprise.

"Request Sadet Chaokhana to take Plang with you," KhunPhraNai said, using Busaba's given name as if they were old acquaintances.

Thien's brow furrowed. It felt like he'd been struck with a bundle of bamboo. If Plang or Busaba was on their side too, why had he opposed every step of his work?

"What does this… mean? I don't understand, sir."

Thien recalled telling KhunPhraNai about Busaba's misdeeds, and KhunPhraNai's advice had been to stay away from him. Now, suddenly, he was to count him as an ally?

Thien swallowed hard, unsure how to proceed. Was he

expected to ally himself with him now, even flatter him as if he were his superior?

"Plang was the first spy sent here," KhunPhraNai said. "But when Sadet Chaokhana began to distance himself from Plang, we decided to bring you in instead."

"Why then…" Thien opened his mouth to ask why Busaba had repeatedly sabotaged his efforts, but KhunPhraNai anticipated him.

"Why did Plang keep undermining you?" he said. "Because when Sadet Chaokhana pulled away, he would suspect you of being the newly planted spy. Plang quarrelled with you on purpose so that the prince wouldn't look at you with suspicion."

Having eased Thien's uncertainty, KhunPhraNai let Busaba step closer to Thien.

"That's why KhunPhraNai couldn't tell you I was on your side," Busaba spoke then, his tone low and masculine, devoid of his usual sweet voice. "If his betrayal were discovered, both you and I would be exposed as well."

Thien's eyes went wide with shock. He dropped onto the nearest bench, breath hitching as a wave of nausea rose in his throat.

Before volunteering for this secret mission, Thien had no idea how dangerous it would be. KhunPhraNai had never asked him to do more than perform Khon and assist the prince closely. But now that he knew Busaba's secret, he understood the stakes of the knowledge he'd been gathering.

If word ever got out that Busaba was the prince's favored confidant…

If the plan to damage the prince's reputation became known…

He now grasped how perilous this mission truly was.

"What must I do, sir?" Thien asked softly, though he only wished to return to his room and sleep, to pretend none of this was real. But he knew it was impossible.

"At dawn, Plang will create an uproar, demanding to come along," KhunPhraNai said. "You must support his request—to avoid any complications."

"I understand," Thien nodded, believing that was all he had to do. He rose from the bench. But KhunPhraNai continued, "One more thing. Once you reach Ayutthaya, you are to deliver the pectoral ornament to Plang."

"What of the pectoral?" Thien frowned. It had disappeared once before, and the prince had recovered and returned it himself. If it were given to Busaba, he would never forgive him.

"You mustn't know," said Busaba abruptly, voice hard.

"If I don't know the reason, I can't comply," Thien replied firmly.

Busaba's expression darkened. "It is better you do not know everything," he repeated.

Thien shook his head vigorously. Having once been his rival, he found it impossible to trust Busaba now, particularly given how much Thien still didn't know.

"It came from an excavation in old Ayutthaya," Busaba said quietly. "It is proof that Sadet Chaokhana plans rebellion."

"What? A single ornament… could that really incite rebellion?" Thien scoffed.

"There are rumors from Ayutthaya that the pectoral unlocks hidden treasure. Whoever owns it could amass enough wealth to overthrow a throne," Busaba said gravely, his words carried the weight of truth.

"If it is so valuable, why give it to me?" Thien asked incredulously. When it was stolen last time, Sadet Chaokhana returned it personally.

There was a moment of silence before KhunPhraNai's voice dropped, sending a chill down Thien's spine: "Clearly, Sadet Chaokhana is leading an expedition to Ayutthaya and you are part of it."

Busaba's warning returned to him. Some knowledge is better left unknown, and keeping this from him had been for his own good.

***

Busaba made a noisy scene, demanding to accompany Prince Khun Luang to Ayutthaya. His voice echoed through the entire Ruen Horton. If it had been before, Thien would've walked away and let her dance around the prince on her own. But now, he simply sat and watched the drama unfold to the very end, alongside Yot, Chuea, and Master Maan, waiting for Sadet Chaokhana to turn and ask for his opinion.

"Thien, what say you?"

"As Your Highness pleases," Thien replied with a respectful bow. "I believe it'll be more fun with a few more people, Your Highness."

The prince's eyes widened, perhaps expecting Thien to object. But when Thien agreed, he gave a brief nod, either to resolve the matter quickly or, possibly, to spare his ears further torment.

Once he had Sadet Chaokhana's permission, Busaba quickly scrambled down from Ruen Horton to pack his belongings, for the boat was scheduled to leave the next day.

Thien also excused himself. But he had not even reached the dormitory when a small hand grabbed his arm and pulled him behind the kitchen.

"Hey. What are you doing, Muan?" he whispered, startled. "Touching me like this, it's not proper."

"Thien!" Muang cried, her face twisted in a deep frown as she said his name.

Thien's heart dropped. He prayed his instinct was wrong, but it wasn't.

"Who are you really? Why did you come here?" she asked, eyes locked on his.

"I don't know what you're talking about," Thien replied, determined not to answer. Even with a knife to his throat, he would not confess.

"If you don't tell me," she threatened, "I'll go straight to Sadet Chaokhana and tell him what I heard last night."

"You've got no proof. I was in the dorm all night, didn't go anywhere."

"Didn't go anywhere? I saw you myself, talking with KhunPhraNai about…" she opened her mouth, but Thien rushed to cover it with his hand.

Muang shook her head, digging her nails into his arm. Still, he wouldn't let go, so she bit down hard. He gritted his teeth and groaned in pain.

"Ow. You bite like a dog!" Thien yanked his hand back. There was a crescent-shaped bite mark bleeding on his palm.

As his hand throbbed, he scrambled for an answer, one that would bring the least harm to anyone.

Luckily, Muang glanced at the wound and seemed to waver. Her eyes softened with pity, torn between two loyalties. One was the master she respected; the other, the man she loved.

She bowed her head and spoke in a trembling voice, "Promise me you won't hurt Sadet Chaokhana. Outsiders may try to ruin him, but you… You're with him every day. You of all people should know he's a good man. Swear it to me. Right here, right now, that you won't harm him."

Tears welled in the corners of her eyes.

Her heart must've been breaking. She had misjudged him, loved the wrong person, and now it was too late. All she could do was beg him to stop whatever plan he was a part of.

Thien reached out to wipe her tears, but instead, it was his own that spilled. Of course, he understood how she felt. But it was too late to turn back now. All he could do was stay afloat and try to ease the damage when the time came.

"I promise," he said.

Chapter 5

The sun had barely risen when a boat with a weathered wooden canopy glided to the pier. It bore no grandeur, yet offered just enough shelter for Prince Khun Luang and his khon troupe on their long passage upriver to Ayutthaya.

Busaba arrived first. He stood right at the water's edge, shifting from foot to foot as if terrified he might be left behind.

Thien came shortly after, walking behind the prince. Sadet Chaokhana had summoned him before dawn to help carry luggage from the sleeping chamber.

Behind Thien came Chuea and Yot, the latter dragging his feet as he lingered to say goodbye to Muang.

Those two had been acting suspiciously close lately, but Thien said nothing. Muang had grown into a young woman. If

Yot's intentions were sincere and truly meant to ask for her hand, it was unlikely Master Maan would object. The young man came from a decent family. Still, marriage would mean leaving the khon troupe. Not that Yot minded; he had never taken to the stage as seriously as others.

Once everyone was aboard, Muang waved from the pier, her gaze lingering on Thien. Her expression was somber due to what had transpired between them the day before.

Thien returned the wave and nodded subtly, assuring her he would keep his promise. Then he turned to glance at Sadet Chaokhana, seated on a raised dais surrounded by guards and servants, his face serene and unreadable.

The barge glided along the Bangkok Noi canal, passed Nonthaburi, and headed for Ayutthaya. Throughout the journey, Busaba kept up a stream of flattery and charm, clearly trying to catch Sadet Chaokhana's attention. Strangely, His Highness did not seem bothered by it.

Thien, on the other hand, sat in moody silence. He couldn't explain his irritation, but it lingered like a shadow. Luckily, Yot filled the hours with chatter and lighthearted games, lifting the tension from the air.

Eventually, their boat turned into the Sra Bua Canal and pulled up beside a large Western-style wooden house. Its hipped roof sloped gracefully beneath the trees, and unlike traditional Thai dwellings, the house stood flat on the ground without a raised platform. The design spoke of modern tastes. Perhaps the owner was someone accustomed to trading with foreigners and adopting their ways.

Each performer was given a private room, which should've felt like a luxury except Yot flat-out refused to sleep alone. He tiptoed after Thien, whining.

"Can I stay with you tonight? What if there's a Portuguese ghost and I can't understand what he's saying?" he whispered.

Thien nearly choked on his laugh. "You're scared of every kind of ghost. Thai, Chinese, and even ones from neighboring countries."

Yot didn't argue. He rolled out his mat beside Thien's like it was the most reasonable thing in the world. Thien sighed. There was no winning against fear, not when it had taken hold of Yot so completely.

The next day was the full moon of the twelfth lunar month. Everyone was called to breakfast. Kitchen servants laid trays of food upon the platform, treating the performers as honored guests.

Oddly, though the prince had instructed his staff to look after everyone well, he himself had left the house early. No one had seen him since.

That afternoon, one of the guards knocked on Thien's door and summoned him to the foreign-language library. At first, Thien assumed it was to help with work. Every time the prince met with senior officials, he would return with letters or royal decrees for Thien to read or help draft responses for.

But when Thien arrived, he found two new figures seated with the prince. He immediately recognized Prince Noppawan, a fellow official in the same department and well-known in the capital for attending nearly every royal function.

The young woman beside him was unfamiliar. She looked younger than the prince, radiant, with soft features, fair skin, and the poise of noble birth. She wore a fine, patterned loincloth and a shawl draped with elegance. She looked even younger than

Thien and couldn't possibly be the prince's consort.

This is Princess Praphaiporn, Prince Noppawan's daughter," Prince Khun Luang introduced. Thien bowed deeply in respect.

The young princess inclined her head modestly, without any hint of disdain. She did not look down on Thien for being a commoner, which instantly warmed him to her.

"So this is the boy who holds the pendant," Prince Noppawan said, his gaze fixed on the ornament resting on Thien's chest. His choice of words was curious, as if Thien were the rightful owner, though the pendant had been a gift from Sadet Chaokhana. By all rights, it still belonged to the prince.

Prince Khun Luang responded only with a nod, choosing not to linger on the subject. Instead, he swiftly changed course.

"I summoned you because I want you to serve as a companion and guardian for my niece tonight. She wishes to attend the lantern festival, but I, along with Prince Noppawan, must preside over the evening's ceremonies. It wouldn't be proper for her to wander through the festivities alone, nor would she enjoy sitting aboard the royal barge all night. There's no one

I trust for this task but you. Will you do it?"

"I would be honored, Your Highness," Thien replied, bowing his head. Out of the corner of his eye, he noticed a blush rising on the princess's cheeks and felt the heat of his own in response.

"Good. After the festivities, take her to the dock where my men will be waiting. The rest of the troupe will return here by hired boat," Prince Khun Luang concluded, his tone brisk and precise, as always.

Shortly after, Prince Khun Luang and Prince Noppawan departed on the royal barge, joined by a procession of noble boats. The only member of the troupe permitted to accompany them was Busaba, who had insisted on going. The others followed in smaller boats, some grumbling under their breath.

Thien, however, found himself aboard a vessel with only the young princess and a single oarsman. The rest of the guards and companions had been assigned to a separate boat. He wasn't sure why the prince had arranged it this way. It could hardly be because of space; there was room enough. More likely, the prince sought to protect the princess's dignity. To be surrounded by young male performers might not befit someone of her rank.

"Have you ever floated a krathong before, Your Highness?" Thien asked gently, breaking the silence that hung between them.

" You can just call me Praphaiporn," she said, her voice light and unpretentious. "I want to enjoy tonight like an ordinary girl."

Thien was taken aback. Apart from his adoptive mother, he had never spoken so informally to a woman of noble blood.

"Yes, Your…Praphaiporn," he corrected himself quickly.

She smiled, clearly pleased. "How about you? Have you ever floated one before, Thien?"

He nodded. "I have. My father used to take my mother and me to the river every year. We made our own krathongs from banana leaves and lit firecrackers. It was my favorite festival." His voice softened. "But since he passed away, my mother and I haven't gone. It just reminds us too much of him."

The princess's smile faded, and her eyes filled with a quiet sympathy. She asked no further questions about his past, steering the conversation to lighter topics until they reached the riverfront, where the celebration had already begun.

Though Thien had never set foot in Ayutthaya before, he had grown up with stories and painted scenes of its glory. He had imagined a faded city, worn by war, left to slumber in quiet decay. But tonight, the old capital shimmered with life.

The riverbanks bloomed with garlands of fresh flowers, their scent wafting through the night air. Bamboo rafts floated gently along the water, built so villagers could place their lanterns with ease. Two open-air theaters stood across from each other, vying for attention. One hosted a Likay troupe, loud and playful, bursting with garish costumes and comic banter. The other featured a more graceful folk play, its singers weaving old verses into soft melodies that drifted over the crowd.

Overhead, Chinese fireworks streaked through the sky, exploding into fans of red, gold, and silver. The night lit up in celebration, rivaling even the grandest festivals of the capital.

As Thien and the princess walked along the shore, weaving between food stalls and boats turned into shops, her eyes lit up at the sight of a sugar blower shaping candy into animals. With a delighted laugh, she dashed over, handed the vendor a few coins, and returned, holding up a monkey-shaped sweet.

She held the candy monkey up beside Thien's face, squinting one eye like an artist sizing up a portrait.

"Uncanny," she declared with a mischievous grin. "The same sulky face, the same furrowed brow. Honestly, if you don't smile right now, I won't be able to tell you two apart."

Thien's lips twitched. He widened his eyes in exaggerated shock, then raised his fingers in a Hanuman mudra and struck a dramatic pose. With perfect comedic timing, he began to hop and twirl to the faint rhythm of the ranat drifting from the nearby likay stage. Each leap was more ridiculous than the last.

The princess clutched her side with laughter.

"You've got it all wrong!" she said between giggles. "This is Ayutthaya, not Lanka! You're attacking the wrong kingdom, oh mighty monkey king!"

"Cheep cheep!" Thien squeaked, dropping the pretense of grandeur entirely. He scrunched up his face like a confused baby monkey, scratched his head, then scampered in a small circle as if trying to find his missing tail.

They both burst into laughter, loud and unguarded. When

they finally caught their breath, Thien offered his arm and guided her toward the temple steps, still grinning like the monkey she claimed he was.

Despite the damage to the ancient walls, the Buddha images remained. People came to pay respects, lighting incense and bowing with reverence—a sign that devotion, like the river, endured.

***

Busaba looked positively smug after getting to ride beside the prince for the entire festival. He had barely stepped off the boat before launching into his usual bragging, telling anyone that some villagers had mistaken him for one of the prince's consorts.

Yot rolled his eyes after hearing the story at least three times already. "Try becoming one first before you strut around like that," he muttered, just loud enough for Thien to hear.

Thien didn't say anything, but he understood the frustration. Busaba wasn't just being bold. There was a sharpness to the way he moved, the way he smiled at the prince, the way he made sure everyone saw. It could've been part of his mission. Maybe he had been told to stir gossip, chip away at the prince's reputation, one rumor at a time. With spies like him, it was never clear what the actual assignment was.

Thien had tried to stay out of it. But the more he watched Busaba act like royalty, the more something twisted inside him. Not quite jealousy, not quite suspicion. Just simmering irritation that made him understand exactly how Yot felt.

So, on the journey back to the capital, Thien slipped in between Sadet Chaokhana and Busaba and gently broached the topic.

"Have you ever composed a phleng yao, Your Highness?"

A phleng yao was a kind of verse once traded between boats, gentle teasing or courtly praise, usually aimed at young ladies sitting by the water or riding in nearby boats.

"A phleng yao? For charming girls?" the prince said, raising a brow with mock seriousness.

"I've heard it's all the rage nowadays, but I've never heard anyone recite one in person, Your Highness."

"You're not going to let me enjoy a quiet evening, are you?" The prince gave a long-suffering sigh, though a smile was already tugging at the corner of his mouth.

Thien could tell he was enjoying himself. A scholar like him would never turn down a chance to show off his way with words.

"Well then," said the prince. "Every verse needs someone to answer. You'll be the maiden, and I'll send my lines across the bow. But you'd better reply. Fair's fair."

There it was…Sadet Chaokhana could never resist a challenge that let his wit shine.

"With pleasure, Your Highness," Thien said with a smirk of satisfaction.

"Are you sure you can even do it?" Busaba cut in, his voice full of doubt.

Thien had never claimed to be a real poet. He only wrote verses for fun, or when trading rhymes with Sadet Chaokhana. Still, the prince smiled, eyes fixed on him with a look that made it hard to breathe.

A phleng yao had rules. It started on the second syllable and ended with oei. Thien had thought about trying it once, just for amusement. But he'd never had anyone he truly wanted to court. This time, though, going back and forth with the prince felt unexpectedly thrilling.

He caught the prince watching him with such warmth in his eyes that Thien suddenly wondered if the prince was picturing him as a lady, the kind a poet might serenade. The thought made his cheeks flush. Before the prince even finished his verse, Thien's face was already red. He grabbed a folding manuscript and scribbled on it, pretending to take notes. Anything to hide how flustered he felt. He couldn't let the prince see just how much the words had gotten to him.

The moment the prince finished with the final oei, Thien spoke quickly, trying to sound composed.

"Your Highness's verse is unmatched. No poet could outshine you."

"I owe it to the time I spent in royal service under the former King, who graciously supported many poets," the prince replied with sincere fondness, his gaze faraway as he recalled the golden age of verse.

Those who cherished khon drama often held great reverence for the art of poetry, as the two were inextricably linked. Without verse, a performance lacked soul.

"Speaking of poetry, dear Praphaiporn wishes for someone to exchange verses with. When we return to the capital, I shall take you to Prince Noppawan's palace. We've been invited for a game of chess. While I am occupied, you may keep her company and compose a few lines together."

His tone was calm. It was not an order, but Thien could tell he meant for him to go. And truth be told, he welcomed the invitation. The young princess was charming and clever. Spending time with her might ease his mind, especially now, when he had yet to decide how to handle Busaba or how far Thien could trust him.

"With gratitude, Your Highness."

"Now then, it is your turn," the prince said with a smile and a slight nod.

Thien opened his mouth to reply, but the words never came. A high-pitched scream sliced through the air. Then the boat lurched.

Wood groaned. Water slapped hard against the hull. Another vessel had slammed into their prow, a roofed one moving far too quickly, its course reckless, almost deliberate. Someone shouted for control. Too late.

The barge tilted violently once and then flipped.

Thien plunged into the canal. Cold swallowed him whole. He kicked upward, broke the surface with a gasp, and coughed river water from his lungs. Chaos reigned around him. Most were already swimming to shore. But Thien spun in the water, scanning faces, searching for one.

"Your Highness!" he cried, voice hoarse. No reply. Only the churning dark below. He inhaled, filled his lungs, and dove. The canal pulled at him, fast and rough. Water swirled past his ears. He blinked through the sting, heart racing, afraid he was already too late.

"Thien!" Yot's voice broke through behind him. Thien surfaced for a second. Yot clung to a broken beam nearby, soaked and wide-eyed. "Are you all right?"

"I'm fine! I still can't find Sadet Chaokhana," Thien shouted back, panic rising. He could see others reaching the riverbank, but not the prince.

He's the enemy, Thien. Let him drown. Save yourself.

His heart thudded wildly. He felt as if something was

tearing open inside him. The image of the prince, lifeless in the water, haunted him.

No. He couldn't abandon him. Even if it meant dying with him, he would not stop searching. Thien plunged back underwater. This time, he dove deeper. The prince was tall. If he had sunk, it would be farther down.

A shadow appeared in the murky depths. Thien forced his eyes open, despite the stinging pain, and prayed silently.

Please be alive. People say you are wise, gifted, and even blessed with supernatural resilience. So why should a simple boat wreck be the end of you?

Thien kicked harder, diving until he swore he would not return to the surface without the prince. Without him, there was no meaning left in Thien's life.

Finally, a glimmer caught his eye. The prince's pendant was shining faintly beneath the water.

The prince's leg was caught in a snarl of roots beneath the water. His arms flailed weakly, bubbles escaping his lips in bursts of panic. Thien dove again, lungs burning, and clawed at the mess of vines and mud. His fingers bled from sharp twigs, but he didn't stop.

At last, the roots gave way. Thien grabbed the prince under the arms and kicked upward with all his strength. They broke the surface together.

The prince gasped, coughing violently. His head lolled for a moment as he fought to breathe, chest rising in stuttering heaves. Thien held him steady, heart thudding with relief.

"Your Highness, are you hurt?"

"I'm all right," the prince rasped. His lips were pale, trembling from the cold. "Get to shore."

Thien nodded, still catching his breath. But just as he turned to swim, a desperate voice tore through the mist.

"Help! Please help!" Busaba's voice. He was clinging to a wooden plank, flailing helplessly. He couldn't swim. The current was dragging him farther from shore.

The prince made a motion to swim toward Busaba, but Thien quickly stopped him.

"Let me go, Your Highness,"

With the prince's permission, Thien swam toward

Busaba, who clung to a drifting plank far from shore. Just as he reached the dancer, Busaba lunged at him in a panic. Arms locked around Thien's shoulders. The sudden weight dragged both of them under.

"Don't! You're pulling me down!" Thien shouted, kicking to keep his head above water. But Busaba thrashed wildly, hitting Thien's ribs and chest, clawing for air.

Water flooded Thien's mouth. The river stung his eyes. He struggled, kicked harder, heart pounding in his ears. He wanted to shake Busaba off. Leave him. Swim to shore and breathe. But he couldn't do it. Instead, he held on and pushed forward, fighting against the combined weight of their bodies and the current.

His arms trembled. His lungs burned. The taste of rot filled his throat. When he finally let go, it wasn't out of choice.

It was because his body had nothing left to give.

Chapter 6

"Thien, please don't hurt Sadet Chaokhana," came the soft voice.

Thien heard it and smiled faintly as if he could ever harm him. He hadn't just spared the prince but offered his life in the process. That alone made him the worst spy imaginable. He had failed his mission and thrown his life away for nothing.

He looked up, only to meet the eyes of his adopted father. Not with anger, but disappointment.

"I beg your forgiveness," Thien whispered. "I was wrong. I couldn't avenge you as I vowed.

He bowed low and pressed his forehead to the feet of the man who had once been his guiding star.

But the elder turned wordlessly and walked away.

Thien tried to call out, but no sound came. Only the far-off voice of Prince Khun Luang reached his ears.

"Take him to Ruen Horton."

"He won't last the night, Your Highness," said the European doctor. His Thai was oddly accented, but clear enough. "He's burning with fever."

"The rowers confirmed it was Consort Ngo's boat, Your Highness, but she wasn't on board. Only her maidservants."

"Whip them all," the prince commanded coldly.

Thien groaned before seeing white clouds.

A bright sun overhead, yet his body felt neither hot nor cold. The pounding in his skull had vanished.

He must be in heaven.

He had never done any great good in life. Aside from infiltrating the palace with the intent to harm the prince, he had committed no true evil either.

Thien rose from the ground just as the elephant spirit reached out his trunk. The second time now. Without protest, Thien climbed onto the gentle giant's back.

"Where will you take me this time?" he asked, stroking the beast's neck.

The elephant walked forward slowly. And then, the light faded to black.

***

Thien jolted awake and found himself on a teak bed with four carved posts, each etched with delicate patterns that made it clear this was no commoner's bed. He immediately scrambled off, crawling down in alarm once he saw the prince seated at one of the posts where the mosquito net was tied.

A commoner shouldn't touch a noble's bed, and yet he'd been sprawled across it who knew how long. The last thing he remembered was sitting beside the prince as he composed a poem aboard the boat.

"Your Highness, I beg Your pardon," Thien said, forehead pressed to the floor. Pain was forgotten. All he could feel now was dread, and the fever sweat soaking through his clothes. He coughed, his throat dry and raw. How had he ended up sleeping on the prince's bed?

He was doomed. If he didn't get whipped, he'd be shamed

for life.

"At last, you're awake." The prince's face relaxed with visible relief.

"Anyone out there?" The prince called toward the door.

Yot, who had been yawning just outside, jumped up.

"Bring some water so he can wash his face," the prince ordered.

"I can do it myself, Your Highness," Thien said quickly.

"No need. Do it here. If you pass out again and hit something, we'll all be in trouble." The powerful voice of Ten-faced Ravana filled the room, impossible to argue with.

The prince left the room after giving the command, and Yot entered with a porcelain basin patterned in blue and rimmed with gold. He placed it before Thien and wrung out a cloth.

"You know how long you were out?" Yot asked, handing over the cloth.

Thien shook his head.

"Two full days. Sadet Chaokhana didn't sleep either. He sat by your side the whole time, wiping you down and keeping watch. Only when your fever finally broke did he go to rest in the writing room. He came back again this morning to check on you. I thought you'd sleep through another day."

"Master Maan offered to care for you, but Sadet Chaokhana refused. You know how stubborn he is. No one can talk sense into him."

"He didn't have to stay."

"He wasn't going to leave. He ordered the court physicians to bring you back, no matter what the cost. It was a royal command. While you were unconscious, no one dared approach him. Even I had to wait outside."

"What about Busaba?" Thien asked.

"What about him?"

"Is he safe?" Thien still couldn't remember if he had gotten Busaba to shore.

"Someone like him? Hell doesn't even want him. Why worry?"

"He said he couldn't swim. I want to know if someone helped him in time."

"What do you mean, can't swim? He grew up on the Mekong. Anyone who believes that lie is an idiot."

A chill ran down Thien's spine. If Busaba could swim, why cry for help? Was he acting?

And what would've happened if the prince had been the one to dive in after him?

"Don't mention Busaba's swimming to Sadet Chaokhana," Thien whispered.

"I couldn't care less about that bastard. Just saying his name makes my mouth taste bitter." Yot picked up the basin and left to change the water.

Thien didn't dare lie back down. He followed Yot out to the sleeping quarters.

Fragments of memory began to return, like scattered petals drifting back to the surface after a storm. He remembered the prince's voice, low but firm, commanding the court physicians to save him no matter the cost. He saw flashes of the senior consort's attendants kneeling by Ruen Horton, pleading tearfully for the prince to return to the palace. His Highness had not budged. Instead, he had dismissed them coldly, his tone sharper than Thien had ever heard.

Another blurred image surfaced. The prince was seated at his bedside, gently coaxing him to swallow spoonfuls of greens boiled to softness. Thien could still taste the broth, plain and bitter, yet somehow more nourishing than any royal banquet. He had been too weak to eat, yet the prince had patiently fed him, one spoonful at a time. Was it a dream or real?

Thien lifted a hand to his lips. Heat rushed to his cheeks.

"Thinking about someone?" a voice teased right beside him.

"Muang! Don't shout like that. You'll make me deaf." He jumped.

"I called and called and you didn't hear, so of course I had to shout. I wanted to pity you since you were sick, but now that I know Princess Praphaiphon came to visit you every single day, I don't pity you one bit. I'm jealous!" Muang held up a plate of rice porridge meant for the sickroom, but once she heard he had recovered, she chased after him.

"What are you talking about? Who said Her Highness visited every day?"

"Don't pretend you don't know. I hate liars." She shoved the porridge into his hands.

"No one told me. And there's nothing between us. Her father only asked me to act as an escort during the Loy Krathong festival."

"I don't believe a word you say anymore," Muang declared, eyes full of resentment.

For the first time, Thien felt a stab of fear. Love that turned to hatred was fierce. When he was a boy, his adoptive mother had warned him: never lead someone on if you don't love them, a woman's love, once betrayed, could become something terrifying.

***

Thien couldn't return to dance practice for several days. Every time he stood, a coughing fit would seize him and refuse to stop. Master Maan eventually ordered him to stay in his room until the cough went away completely, which also meant he couldn't assist the prince with official duties.

"Don't worry about it," Yot told him, ever the messenger. "Sadet Chaokhana hasn't been to the Ruen Horton in days anyway."

Though Thien remained confined indoors, Yot came daily with news.

"They say he had a falling out with Consort Ngo, ever since he gave the order to have her maidservants whipped. She reported it straight to His Majesty. Caused a real uproar."

"It reached the King?" Thien swallowed hard.

"You didn't know who Consort Ngo is, did you? She's the daughter of the Grand Chancellor. Jealous as hell. When she heard that Sadet Chaokhana was going to float krathongs with Busaba, she completely lost it. Ordered her servants to take a boat and wait at the river junction. Then, he told the oarsmen to ram straight into Sadet Chaokhana's prow."

Busaba again… Thien thought bitterly.

"Anyway, what happened between you and Muang?" Yot asked. "I told her to come visit you, but she refused. Said she doesn't like liars. What did you lie to her about?"

"Nothing," Thien answered quickly, shaking his head.

"She's been waiting for Sadet Chaokhana to return, too.

Said she's going to report what you and Busaba were up to."

Yot scratched his head, looking puzzled.

Thien felt a knot in his chest. He lay awake for nights, wondering how to stop Muang from talking. She wasn't just avoiding him but refused to listen to anything he said.

Maybe it was time to leave before everything came crashing down.

***

Whispers of a khon dancer accompanying the prince during the Loy Krathong festival spread swiftly beyond palace walls, fueling outrage from Consort Ngo. Yet the King issued no censure, no rebuke. Unlike the usual scandals that left royal consorts disgraced, this one met only silence. And that silence was telling. It unsettled his rivals more than any decree could, confirming what many feared: the prince's power was still very much intact.

More than a month passed before the prince finally returned to the Horton Pavilion. As soon as Thien heard the news, he rushed to pay his respects, hoping to arrive before Muang could cause trouble, but he was too late. She was already there, seated beside Sadet Chaokhana on the dais in the main hall. When she spotted Thien entering, she cast him a cutting glance before excusing herself and leaving.

Thien dropped to his knees and performed a formal five-point prostration, his forehead touching the floor. But the prince did not acknowledge the gesture. Instead, he rose to his feet and retreated to his private quarters, shutting the door with a firm bolt.

Thien remained kneeling long after the prince had vanished from sight. Shame coursed through his skin like fever. He had risked everything to protect His Highness that day on the river, but it hadn't been enough. The prince now knew who he truly was. Or rather, who he had once been sent to be.

He had lied. He had betrayed the one man who had shown him unexpected kindness.

***

For the next few days, Thien wasn't summoned. Only Muang came to relay orders at his door. "Sadet Chaokhana said you needn't come to Ruen Horton unless summoned," she declared flatly. That left Thien with no chance to explain himself.

Meanwhile, Busaba continued going up and down from

Ruen Horton as if nothing had happened.

"Muang… did Sadet Chaokana ask for me today?" Thien asked as he did every day—not just for an answer, but hoping to mend things with her. She hadn't returned to dance practice by the rice fields either.

"No idea," she replied with a shake of her head.

"Are you still angry at me? I've told you. I never intended to harm Sadet Chaokana. If I were lying, why would I dive into the water to save him that day?" he whispered, taking the chance to speak while she was eating alone outside the canteen.

"No more excuses," she snapped. "Go explain yourself to Sadet Chaokana if you must." Still, her anger seemed to have softened slightly. This time, she didn't walk away.

"But… what exactly did you tell him? Why can Busaba meet him freely, but I can't?"

"Who said you can't?" she shot back. "If you want to go, just go. No one's stopping you."

"But you said he ordered I shouldn't go up unless summoned."

"He said that day he was tired and wanted rest. I didn't say anything about other days."

"What!" Thien's voice rose in frustration. He glanced toward Ruen Horton. How many days had he wasted, thinking the door was shut to him?

"Well, I'm telling you now, aren't I? Go on then," she said, teasingly.

Without waiting, Thien dashed off toward Ruen Horton.

He found the prince seated in the writing room, quill in hand. The prince placed the feather pen down and turned to face him, expression unreadable. Thien wisely held his tongue.

"Gone for days. Just because I didn't summon you, you vanish completely?"

"I accept whatever punishment Your Highness sees fit… Muang told me not to show my face unless you called, Your Highness."

"And since when does Muang give you orders?"

He's in real trouble now, Thien thought grimly, gritting his teeth.

"It was my own misunderstanding, Your Highness," he admitted, bowing once more.

"Come walk with me," the prince said, standing and reaching for his sword before leading Thien down Ruen Horton steps.

Yot, who had been chatting with Muang near the kitchen, stared wide-eyed as they passed. The prince never used this route. He usually walked toward the theatre instead of crossing the canal. But Thien knew. The prince wasn't heading to the dock.

He pushed through banana leaves until they reached Muang's old secret hideout. No longer so hidden.

Well… this is it, Thien thought. But though he sensed the end approaching, he didn't flee. He knelt beside the platform where the prince now sat, gazing across the golden fields.

"You once said you were an orphan," the prince said, turning to face him. "Tell me again. Who was your guardian?"

It felt like a courtroom interrogation. Thien inhaled deeply, trying to figure out how to answer without implicating anyone else. Not even Busaba.

This must be what it feels like when a spy has failed his

mission…

"My foster father once served in the Ministry of Defense," Thien said carefully.

The prince, unimpressed, slowly drew his sword and placed its gleaming edge against Thien's neck. Not to wound. Just to make a point. It worked.

"His name?" came the soft but firm question.

Thien shut his eyes, took a breath, and answered clearly.

"ChaoKhun Phut, Your Highness."

"He wasted away in prison," the prince said, as if recalling an old friend.

Thien bowed his head, unable to hold back a sarcastic edge to his tone. "You remember him, then?"

"Of course I do. A great pity. He was honest and sharp-witted—a scholar of Siam. None could match his command of verse. No wonder you learned poetry."

Thien didn't know all the details of the past, but hearing his father's enemy speak of him with such respect brought tears to his eyes. Whether from sorrow or rage, he couldn't tell. It all blurred now.

The prince sheathed the sword and set it carelessly on the platform. Then he stepped closer and looked down at Thien. Not with hostility, but with a gaze that said plainly, *'I never saw you or your father as an enemy.'*

"Is that why you and Plang wanted me dead?"

"No, Your Highness," Thien said firmly. "I had no part in the boat attack. If you suspect me, then strike me down now. Kill me here with your blade and throw my body into the moat. Let your hand not be stained."

He pressed his forehead to the earth, tears soaking into the dirt. Eyes closed, he thought of his mother, his father, and all who had shown him kindness.

He'd failed them all. But if he lived again, in another life, he would repay every debt.

"Get up. Go wash, pack your things. We leave tonight. Bring the pendant I gave you. Meet me at the landing by the theatre."

The prince picked up his sword, leading the way.

Thien wiped his tears and looked confused, but didn't argue. At least for now, his head was still attached, and all his limbs remained intact.

Chapter 7

By the time Thien reached the river landing, the prince's boat was already waiting, its curved roof glinting faintly in the fading light. Beneath the dock pavilion, the prince reclined in a low wooden chair, legs crossed casually, draped in layers of pale silk and a neatly pleated jongkraben. The double robe clung to him like mist, soft and subtle, in contrast to the curling smoke between his fingers.

He drew once more from a cigar wrapped in dried banana leaf, the scent of tobacco and leaf fire mingling in the cool air. Then, without ceremony, he flicked the smoldering stub into the river.

A prince should have been still, dignified, and composed. But in that moment, with his rumpled robe, bare feet, and the way he eyed Thien with a smirk that gave nothing away, he looked more like a gang leader staking claim to a dockside alley than a son of kings.

And yet, somehow, he was still magnificent.

"Did you bring it?" His rough voice matched the clothes he wore and sounded like an underworld boss.

Thien couldn't help but smile at the change.

"Yes, Your Highness," he said, handing over a silver box.

The prince took it without a word but did not open it until they were on the boat. Then he placed it beside him on a low wooden bench, not saying anything more.

"From now on, drop the court language. Call me Phi (Brother) Thep. Get used to it. Don't slip up," he added, with a sideways glance.

"Yes, Your Hi—" Thien caught himself, pressed a hand to his mouth, then corrected himself with a playful grin.

"All right… Phi Thep."

Satisfied, the prince stepped into the boat. Two Chinese oarsmen stood at the bow and stern. A lamp glowed inside the cabin, though twilight had yet to fall. There were no attendants, just the prince and Thien. Only then did Thien realize this wasn't the elegant royal barge. It was smaller, worn, with scuffed sides and wood darkened by years on the river.

The oarsmen guided them downriver toward the Chao Phraya, retracing the route to Ayutthaya. The boat glided through the night, neither of them sleeping. Thien nodded off once but snapped himself awake in time.

Phi Thep seemed far from drowsy, still studying a small slip of paper covered in handwritten verse. Thien dared not fall asleep before him, not when the prince was wide awake.

He cleared his throat to break the silence before the weight of his eyelids won.

"What are you reading, Phi Thep? That single page's kept your eyes the whole night."

The prince glanced up and handed it over. Thien unfolded it and began to read aloud, his voice soft but clear in the hush between them.

Toward Sri Sanphet's height the path was led,

Past seven betels, bought as the journey sped.

A longboat bore ten oarsmen, firm of frame,

Six rowed upstream — now heap the firebrand's flame.

When Thien accompanied Princess Praphaiphon to pay respects at the temple, he saw the Three Brother Chedis at Wat Si Sanphet and the twin areca palms lining the path. At first, the verse inscribed on the pendant seemed like a typical nostalgic poem, but as he read on, he realized the second stanza had no relation to the first—its lines were bound only by rhyme, not meaning. He looked up at the prince in puzzlement.

"A clue in verse," Prince Khun Luang said flatly.

Thien's eyes widened. He echoed the phrase in a whisper, lowering his voice instinctively, afraid the boatmen might overhear.

"A clue in verse?"

"Don't worry. The rowers are Lu Ma's men. They're not fluent in Siamese."

This boat must have been borrowed from Sia Lu Ma, indicating that the merchant was involved in this journey from the outset.

"I received this map from Lu Ma himself. His grandfather used to purchase relics and treasures from gold mining concessions during the Thonburi era. This poem was hidden in the same chest as the pendant I gave you."

This verse… It could be the last missing piece that the royal inspector had been seeking.

"You knew I wasn't your ally, merely a thorn in your side. So why would you reveal the secret of the poem to me?"

"And you?" the prince asked. "You knew I had discovered everything. Why didn't you flee with the pendant? Why bring it back to me?" Their eyes met for a long, silent moment, as if neither wanted to yield. But in the end, it was Thien who lowered his gaze first.

"Since the day Your Highness offered me betel nut with your own hand," he said, deliberately switching to formal speech to show his sincerity, "I have ceased to see you as an enemy."

"I have never once seen you or your foster father as enemies," the prince replied. "Your father's death was a tragedy no one foresaw. The punishment was intended as a warning. Nothing more. No one expected that a man so bold with words would be so quick to take his own life before the court even ruled on his innocence."

It was hard to accept such a rebuke of his benefactor, especially from someone he had once considered an adversary. Thien flinched, struggling to compose himself. But gradually, the truth in the prince's words began to take root.

"Why did you bring me along on this journey? I returned the pendant willingly and asked for nothing in return."

He had already returned the treasure. What he still didn't understand was why the prince hadn't killed him or simply cast him aside. What use was there in keeping a sharp blade so close to one's heart?

"Do you remember what I told you about the treasure always finding its way back to its true owner?"

Thien nodded.

"The one who stole your pendant was Plang. I found out when he was screaming in his quarters, burning with fever and pulling out his hair."

Busaba's head wasn't entirely bald as the servants had teased, but he had lost more than a few patches. The prince continued:

"I summoned him and questioned him. The day you saw me with him, I had to threaten him for a long time before he agreed to return it."

"But you have the pendant back now." Thien glanced at the box on the table beside the prince's arm. The silver case, dulled by time, still retained its quiet elegance.

"Yes, but I'm not its true owner. You are, Thien."

Thien's brows rose in disbelief. He was an orphan. Never owned anything of value. And now someone was telling him that he possessed a golden heirloom tied to a treasure that might be worth enough to topple the realm? His heart pounded, sweat beading along his temples.

"They say the buried riches of Ayutthaya can only be

unearthed by a direct descendant of the one who hid them or their reincarnation. Anyone else who tries will be cursed, even royalty."

"How can we prove who the rightful heir or reincarnation is?" Thien asked, still unconvinced.

"That's why I brought you," the prince replied, offering the box to him once again.

Thien took it, opening it carefully to study the design on the pendant's case. Four smaller prangs surrounded a large central one. He had thought it beautiful, but upon closer inspection, he was struck by the goldsmith's meticulous craftsmanship. Silver and gold twisted upward into spired peaks like a miniature temple compound.

"But we still need to decode the verse first, don't we?"

The prince turned to him with a look of quiet admiration. He was clearly pleased that Thien was focused on the task, rather than bitter over his foster father's fate. '

"'Toward Sri Sanphet's height the path was led, Past seven betels, bought as the journey sped. A longboat bore ten oarsmen, firm of frame, Six rowed upstream — now heap the firebrand's flame' Every stanza hides a number. Even the first line, which doesn't mention any figure but if you've ever visited Wat Si Sanphet, you'd know there are three main chedis."

"That's what I thought too," the prince said. "Three chedis, seven betels, ten oarsmen, and rowing six strokes. All together, that makes twenty-six."

"No. It's not twenty- six," Thien said firmly. "If there are ten rowers and they row six times, that's sixty strokes. Add the rest, and it's seventy."

He didn't know why he was so certain. But the number seventy had come to him unbidden—instinctive. If he truly was the treasure's heir, shouldn't he feel it in his bones?

He turned to look again at the pendant—four small prangs, circling a larger one at the center. Princess Praphaiphon had once described a temple where corner prangs encircled the main hall. Could it be the same?

"Have you ever been to Wat Chaiwatthanaram? Do the prangs there match the layout on the pendant?" He passed the box back. The prince's eyes widened. Thien had never seen the temple with his own eyes, but he had, and he remembered it well.

The pendant was a perfect miniature of the layout, with the central tower surrounded by satellite chedis. Not a single detail was amiss.

The stone prangs, once standing proudly like sacred ramparts encircling the celestial Chedi Chulamani atop Mount Meru, now lay in ruin. Ravaged by cannon fire and desecrated by human hands, they had been stripped of their golden crowns and decapitated of their Buddha heads. What grandeur they once held had long since been reduced to crumbling remnants of glory. Even so, the highest prang of Ayutthaya continues to tower above the surrounding ruins.

The prince instructed the two Chinese rowers to measure the base of Wat Chaiwatthanaram's main prang all the way to its highest point. The result confirmed what Thien had long suspected.

"Chik-jab," one of them said. It measured seventy sok. Thien glanced at the prince, who nodded with quiet satisfaction.

It was now certain: this was the site tied to the pendant. The key to the buried treasure. The question that remained was how to uncover it.

***

The prince instructed the men to return the boat to the Sra Bua Canal palace. The rowers, exhausted from the long journey, soon scattered to their sleeping quarters.

Thien had planned to do the same, but as he passed the writing chamber, he saw the prince still at the desk and quietly stepped in.

The prince had fallen asleep in the chair, his fingers still loosely holding the quill, as if caught mid-thought, trying to capture the ancient temple's layout before it faded from memory. His face in slumber looked so youthful, so serene, Thien couldn't help but smile.

They all said the prince was as fierce as the Giant Tosakanth, but the more Thien knew him, the more he resembled the Hero Phra Ram instead. Refined in feature, razor-sharp in mind, precise in every endeavor… *Was he truly as cunning and power-hungry as others claimed?*

Thien rested his chin on his hand and gazed at him, not realizing he had dozed off, slumped against the edge of the desk.

When he woke again, he was lying in bed, warm and blanketed. But this time, he was conscious of being carried. So he pretended to sleep.

The prince had laid him down gently. His footsteps were soft, almost divine, heading toward the door. But then… something made him pause.

Thien's heart fluttered as he heard those footsteps return. He squeezed his eyes shut.

And then he felt it.

The prince's lips pressed lightly against his forehead.

His whole face burned. Inside, he chanted silently, as if it were a mantra.

Please don't let the prince notice…

Please don't let the prince know…how much joy that brought him.

***

Ayutthaya, like the royal capital, slumbered under the sun and came alive by moonlight. By nightfall, the city bustled with life. Canoes floated through the canals before dawn, peddling steamed buns and grilled fish. At dusk, the riverbanks came alive with stalls selling snake wine, dried goods, and sizzling meats through the night.

The prince had shed his noble skin and transformed into a rakish wanderer. Dressed in a jongkaben and carrying a blade at his hip, he puffed on a hand-rolled cheroot and led Thien deep into a tavern near the Portuguese quarter.

A few Moorish and Chinese men lounged about, sipping arak and whispering to Siamese courtesans with surprising fluency, as if they'd been born in the kingdom.

"Don't stare," the prince snapped under his breath, dragging Thien around the back.

The rear of the tavern was a maze of curtained rooms. Some doors ajar, others tightly closed. Those that were open were veiled by beaded curtains, faint plumes of opium smoke curling out to greet them. The scent was unmistakable.

"I thought all the opium dens were shut down," Thien whispered, heart pounding.

"They are. All the ones we don't control," the prince murmured back, exhaling smoke into Thien's face. "Rebel whispers, Chinese secrets. They all start in places like this."

"Brother Thep! It's been a while," the tavern owner called out warmly. He spoke fluent Thai, but his pale skin, tall frame, and sharply defined features revealed his mixed heritage, likely part Portuguese, part Siamese. Most Portuguese settlers still scorned such lineage, referring to the Siamese as their servants and condemning intermarriage. But deep down, it wasn't only bloodlines they feared losing. It was faith. They wanted the Siamese to convert, not to dilute Catholicism into the folds of Buddhism and forget where it came from.

"Busy night," the prince said with casual ease, glancing around the smoky room.

"A trade barge docked two nights ago," the owner replied, his tone suddenly more guarded.

"Anything… interesting?" the prince asked, his voice lowering just slightly.

"Let's talk inside." The tavern keeper gave a short bow and moved to open a door at the back. Before stepping through, he turned to one of his men nearby and gave a nod. "Take his brother to the front and see that he gets something to eat."

The man looked at Thien with a knowing grin. "This one?"

"Yes, that one," the prince answered without looking back.

***

Moments later, Thien found himself seated at a wooden table in the smoky main hall. A man appeared beside him with a grin, setting down a delicate blue-and-white porcelain cup filled with cloudy, pale golden liquor. Inside the jar behind it, a snake coiled in the brine, its fangs frozen mid-snarl.

Thien's stomach turned. He recoiled with a sharp shake of his head. The man shrugged and brought him a cup of rice moonshine instead. Even then, Thien only stared at it. The raw smell of alcohol coiled in his nostrils, untouched.

"First time, isn't it?" A low, teasing voice purred beside him. A courtesan with bold lips and sharper eyes slid into the seat next to him, her body grazing his shoulder. Her gaze swept over him with hungry delight, as if she were choosing how best to devour him.

Thien gave a tight nod and turned away, hoping his silence

would be enough to send her off. But instead, the room went black. A rough cloth bag slammed down over his head, plunging him into darkness.

"Hey!" he shouted, but a broad hand clamped over his mouth. Two powerful arms hooked under his knees and shoulders. He kicked, but the arms held firm. No one in the tavern moved. No one shouted. He was lifted off the floor and carried through the back like a sack of grain. The rush of night air hit his skin just as his captors tossed him into a narrow wooden boat.

The cloth yanked off. Thien squinted against the dim lamplight and saw a familiar, unwelcome face.

"Plang!" he shouted.

But another voice cut in, firm and familiar.

"Enough. Just get it done. We don't have much time."

Thien twisted around, heart thudding. Seated in the center of the boat like a man expecting tribute was none other than KhunPhraNai. Beside him, a Hindu Brahmin in layered, ash-white robes sat still as stone, and on his other flank stood the bodyguard Thien had seen countless times at his side.

The henchmen who had abducted Thien earlier clambered aboard, filling the boat. With that, the rowers began their strokes.

"Where are we going?" Thien asked warily.

"To retrieve the pendant," KhunPhraNai replied. The answer did little to dispel Thien's confusion, but he was the superior. There was no choice but to obey.

Thien was then taken back to retrieve the pendant from Prince Khun Luang's residence, under the watchful eye of Busaba, who never left his side until they returned to the boat.

The rowers guided them toward the ancient prang according to the directions from the treasure poem. The aged Brahmin took the pendant and made his way to the northern face of the towering prang.

"Were you tailing us from the capital?" Thien asked, unable to contain his suspicion any longer. It seemed neither side fully trusted him now. A two-headed snake might be useful, but never trustworthy.

"I kept it from you so you wouldn't tip off Sadet Chaokhana," KhunPhraNai replied, perhaps guessing Thien's thoughts.

Thien sighed. On either side of him now stood KhunPhraNai and the same thug who'd abducted him earlier.

The Brahmin took out a silver tray, unwrapped some coconut dumplings meant for the spirits, and placed them in neat rows. Once the moon had risen to its zenith, he lit a candle. One of the former rowers sat beside him with a spade at the ready. When the candle had burned to its end, the Brahmin nodded. The digger began working. The soil around the prang was black and soft, but not long after, his spade struck a tougher layer of mixed gravel and crushed glass—a sign of a ceremonial burial ground.

Then, the Brahmin turned and motioned for Thien to come forward. Thien stepped beside him, knelt, and paid his respects to the ancient prang. Not entirely conscious of what he was doing, as if by instinct.

"Here, hold this, and repeat after me," the Brahmin said, handing the pendant back.

Thien joined his palms, mimicking the priest's posture.

"I, say your name…" the Brahmin prompted.

"I, Thien…" he replied, adjusting his seat.

"···seek permission as the former owner or a descendant thereof…" At this, Thien's eyes widened. The incense had long since burned out, but its scent still clung to the air, unnervingly strong. "…to uncover this buried treasure. May the guardian spirits open the way for me."

As soon as he finished reciting the words, a flash of light flared from the ground. Thien sprang to his feet in alarm.

The digger raised his tools again, striking harder. The Brahmin continued his chant. Thunder rumbled across the sky despite no sign of clouds earlier. Thien turned to KhunPhraNai, who whispered something to Plang with a satisfied smile.

What will he say to Busaba that he won't say to him? Thien glanced between the Brahmin and KhunPhraNai.

Who did this treasure truly belong to? Prince Khun Luang had claimed more than once that it was Thien's. But if it were unearthed, whose hands would it fall into? His mind spiraled in circles until a chilling trumpeting of an elephant broke through. The same cry he'd once heard in a dream.

Clutching the pendant, he bolted. At first, he crept cautiously, but once he sensed distance, he sprinted with everything he had. The ground quaked beneath his feet. The elephant's cry thundered through the ruined temple, just as it had at the Ruen Horton. But now, it wasn't only he who heard it. Everyone present froze in place, exchanging anxious glances.

"Thien!" KhunPhraNai shouted after him.

He didn't stop. He made for the river, intending to steal a boat and flee. But when he reached it, doubt crept in. Could he even row it alone?

Panting, heart pounding, he thought surely he'd be killed for this betrayal.

"Thien! Over here!" came a familiar voice.

Prince Khun Luang paddled his skiff close to shore. Without hesitation, Thien dashed toward him and helped push the boat off to gain speed. The elephant's cry still echoed. The ground still shook. Screams rang out behind them as if someone had been trampled. Dust clouded the temple ruins. The sky darkened unnaturally.

"He does not grant permission," the prince said quietly, his eyes fixed on the receding shore.

"I don't understand," Thien said, shaking his head.

"We'll talk once we're back at the house."

Fortunately, the current favored their direction, and it didn't take long. Still, Thien felt ashamed as he watched the prince row.

"May I row instead, Your Highness?"

"What, afraid I'll capsize us?" the prince teased.

"No, but it's improper for Your Highness to row while a servant just sits."

"Then call me Phi Thep like I told you—no more titles. Or I'll knock your head with this paddle," he threatened, lifting the oar in jest.

Thien ducked quickly, grinning despite himself.

Chapter 8

The moment they entered Sra Bua Canal Palace, the prince moved swiftly through shadowed corridors, passing stained-glass windows that cast colored light onto the polished floor. At the end of the hall, he stopped before a narrow wooden door, flung it open, and pulled Thien in behind him, slamming it shut with a final, echoing thud. The air inside the library was thick with the scent of old parchment and the smoke of oil lamps. A single lantern flickered in the corner, casting restless shadows across the prince's face.

"What exactly is this treasure, Your Highness?" Thien asked, voice tighter than he meant. "And who does it belong to?"

He could still hear the priest's voice echoing in his skull, naming him the one who must speak the chant to unlock the grave.

"It's not about who owns it. It's about who you're willing to give it to."

He had told Thien before: the pendant would remain with its rightful owner. And now, it was still in Thien's hand. His fingers wrapped tight around the box as if letting go meant losing something far greater than gold.

"Do you want the treasure, Your Highness?"

"I do."

"But… a prince shouldn't hoard wealth or gather power like a warlord."

"Is it only ministers who are allowed to hoard wealth and men?" the prince snapped. "You think the man you serve is more loyal to this country than I am?"

"Hoarding wealth and men is treason, Your Highness."

"I don't intend to overthrow the throne, if that's what you're worried about." the prince's voice lowered. "I only want to protect myself. And my people. That includes you."

Thien shook his head. "A rebellion. Even in self-defense, it is still rebellion."

"You're not me," the prince said softly, but firmly. "You don't understand what it takes to survive in my place. If I don't fight, I'll have to flee into monkhood. Otherwise, one day I'll be accused of treason and rot in a prison cell, just like your foster father." He pointed a finger toward Thien's chest.

Thien met his eyes, confusion flickering through him. He slowly sank to his knees but said nothing.

"Our lives aren't the same, Thien," the prince said, voice grave. "A weak king becomes a puppet for greedy nobles. To rule, a king must be strong. The treasure is meant for someone with power and merit. Anyone else who touches it will only bring ruin upon themselves."

He took a step closer.

"You are the one holding it now. And they know it. If you plan to hand it over to them… then go. I won't stop you. But after that, you're no longer welcome here."

For the first time, the prince's voice turned cold, laced with something that felt like sorrow disguised as a warning. Then he softened.

"You can't return to the Khon troupe. Think carefully." With that, the prince opened the door and left.

***

Thien couldn't sleep that night. He sat alone, debating which side to choose. Freedom was just one step away. All he had to do was walk out of the prince's palace, deliver the treasure to KhunPhraNai, and his mission would be complete. The revenge would be his.

But why did his heart feel sad?

Oh…because he had fallen in love with the enemy, that's why! And now, he couldn't lift a hand against Prince Khun Luang.

At dawn, the prince summoned a company of troops from Ayutthaya's governor to guard the palace. Not to imprison Thien but to protect him.

"If you want to leave, no one will stop you," the prince said when Thien emerged from the chamber. "I've prepared a boat. Once you reach the river's edge, someone will meet you and guide you safely." the prince's eyes were shadowed. He, too, hadn't slept.

"Is there anyone left who worries for me like you do, Your Highness?" Thien asked. "Even on the day I might leave you, you make sure I have a boat to return safely."

"Spare me the words," the prince muttered. "The only thing I regret is losing that sharp tongue of yours. No one else dares trade verses with me like you do."

He stepped aside, leaving the path open. But Thien didn't move.

"May I ask you one more thing, Your Highness?" he said, lifting his eyes. No longer as a servant, but as the brotherly Thien the prince once knew. The prince gave a slow nod.

"That night, when Consort Ngo came to call you at the tower… why didn't you go?"

There was no need to say which night. It was the night Thien nearly died. The night the prince never left his side.

"Consort Ngo is the daughter of a powerful minister. They sent her to my bed, hoping that if I became the heir, their daughter would hold the reins. But when I refused to raise her rank, they grew displeased. They wanted me gone." He turned to the window, checking for signs of anyone waiting. "If I must live under someone's power, let it be His Majesty the King and not those corrupt officials who only serve themselves."

And at last, Thien understood.

To become king was not just about blood. It was about strength. A king ruled not by birthright alone, but by resisting those who would use him like a pawn. The prince didn't crave the throne. He craved a council of good men who wouldn't rob the kingdom blind.

Thien stepped forward, knelt, and pressed his forehead to the prince's feet in a benchapradit bow.

"I no longer wish to be the owner of the pendant," he said. "Let me just be your foul-mouthed Thien, if you'll have me."

He held out the silver box with both hands, voice unwavering.

***

Eight Years Later

Full Moon, 12th Month, Chula Sakarat 1212

To my mangy mutt, Thien,

I sent you off to marry Princess Praphaiphon, thinking by now you'd have given me a dozen grandnephews to spoil. I was disappointed when I heard she complained that you're always working. What work could be more important than your wedding bed? Don't follow my example, for your own sake. Grow old alone like I did, and you'll know what it means to be lonely, with no children to wipe your sweat or call your name.

Things here in the capital are still a mess, but you've moved to the provinces now. That's no longer your concern. Stay out of it.

Last time you sent me a verse to continue…What kind of poem ends every line in a dead syllable? This is all I could come up with. Let's see if you can top it, axe-mouth.

The opera girl from Paet Riw danced herself hungry,

Old Miss Sae-Liw fished for minnows in soy-brine fury…

Khon Spy Behind the Fallen Prince

Princess Praphaiphon stirred the wok with a growling belly,

Ran like the wind, silk flying, bags swinging in a flurry.

Tonight's the Festival of Lights. I didn't float a krathong elsewhere. Can't stand all the gossip. But I do regret never floating one with you. Still, at least you did with Princess Praphaiphon. That means your fates were tied, doesn't it?

In any case, may you live long, stay safe, and avoid harm. If I'm still alive when your child is born, I'll come see you. Maybe even bring a gift to welcome the little rascal.

Thinking of you always,

Your Brother, Khun Luang.

Thien read the final letter from the prince, and every time he did, he found himself wiping away tears. No matter how many years passed, the sorrow never truly faded.

The day Prince Khun Luang passed from this world, the sky turned a blood-red hue that lingered far longer than usual.

Children in the neighborhood cried out as if the heavens themselves mourned.

He and Princess Praphaiphon had been rowing along the canal in front of their home when a baby's cry pierced the dusk. They turned and found a cloth bundle near the water's edge. Thien paddled to shore, and the princess stepped down to lift the child from the reeds.

"What a strange little face," she said softly, brushing a leaf from the boy's brow. Her smile, though, betrayed no revulsion, only tenderness.

Unwrapping the cloth, they found a baby boy, handsome even in infancy. Something in his features whispered of noble blood. Why he had been left by the canal was a mystery they would never solve.

"Then let's raise him as our own, shall we, my lady?" Thien still spoke to her with formality, even years into their marriage.

After Thien chose not to return to KhunPhraNai, the prince quietly sent him to hide in Phitsanulok, a city governed by Princess Praphaiphon's father. It was a safe haven, far from spies or schemers who might kidnap Thien to force open the royal treasure vault.

Officially, Thien had vanished. His name was erased from the court's Khon troupe records, his service forgotten. Only the prince knew the truth.

Thien had taken a new name, Chinnakarn, and become husband to the princess.

But soon after they returned home with the orphaned child, news reached them. A royal courier arrived bearing a sealed decree. The prince was stripped of his royal rank and was slain by decree of the king. The court had declared him guilty of keeping a great number of male khon performers, choosing to share his bed only with them and never with the consorts of the palace. Multiple khon performers were interrogated including Busaba, and their testimonies concurred.

Thien nearly collapsed. Princess Praphaiphon helped him inside and held him as he wept, longer than he ever had, even for the foster father who had raised him.

Only those in power can write history. The prince had gathered strength not for conquest, but for survival. But in the end, power had turned against him just as it had killed Thien's own father, who had died unjudged.

That night, Thien dreamed of the prince visiting him at home. The prince smiled and said, "The world of power, of heirs and enemies, is one you were never meant to understand. But don't grieve. Let's say I paid the debt owed to your father so that you may find peace."

No one dared speak his name again, not in the royal city, nor in the Khun Luang household, which stood as a wedding gift, built by the prince's own hand.

Thien folded the letter, whispering silently in his heart:

At the very least, the prince never lived under any power but that of the King, his only true master.

Part Two – Reincarnation

Chapter 9

Bangkok, Present Day

The royal cremation grounds, once known as Thung Phra Meru, had become Sanam Luang, and the riverside palace, Thapra, had evolved into one of the most prestigious universities in the country. The entire district had changed so much that few would believe it was once all rice paddies. And yet, Ruen Horton, the ancestral Thai house, had remained untouched since the day Great-Grandfather Thien passed away, until today, when his great-grandson was finally forced to sell it.

"Dad, Great-Grandpa Thien was stunning, wasn't he?" said Shinakal, a sharp-featured twenty-year-old in torn jeans that made him look younger than his age. "If he were born in this era, he'd be a BL drama idol for sure. Just look at that bone structure.

Gorgeous as a woman, dashing as a man. No way any filler clinic would make a cent off him."

"Watch that mouth, you rascal," his father, Danai, snapped, rapping him lightly on the head before dusting the framed photo of the house's former master.

"I'm serious. I'm complimenting him!" Shinakal grinned, then wandered deeper into the house he'd inherited from Grandfather Udom two years prior.

Ruen Horton was a traditional Thai house raised on stilts. Danai once told him the original owner had been a Khon master during the early Rattanakosin period. His ashes were still enshrined in the house, next to a portrait of him dressed as a Khon Character, Busaba. His ornate costume glittered with jewels so intricate that no modern artisan could easily replicate it.

At first glance, Shinakal mistook the photo for that of his great-great-grandmother. The man's beauty was striking, with arched brows, lips tinted red, and a tall chatra crown perched elegantly on his head. His father corrected him: "That's Grandpa Thien. He adopted Grandpa Udom as his foster son."

"This photo was taken when he taught Khon in

Phitsanulok, before he moved into this house," Danai had said.

Now that the home had passed to Shinakal, he realized he could no longer afford to preserve it. Living costs in Bangkok were too high, and master artisans capable of repairing it were scarce and few.

"It's a shame, Dad," he admitted. "But if we can't take care of it, maybe selling it to someone who can is the right thing."

They were cleaning the place today because Phonphon, a former schoolmate turned real estate agent, had arranged a visit from a nobleman interested in buying the home. The noble had a habit of collecting old houses in Bangkok and had expressed interest in this one.

"Back then, Grandpa Udom told me there used to be a Khon theatre next door," Danai said, brushing dust from the railing as he gazed beyond the porch. "But after the troupe disbanded, a Chinese investor bought the land and built a hotel. All that's left is this house. Your great-grandfather never agreed to sell it, no matter the offer."

From where they stood, the view stretched across the back garden to the river, where the silhouette of a luxury hotel now loomed through a thinning curtain of trees. The old Thai house seemed to shrink in its shadow, stubbornly clinging to the past.

Shinakal wandered to the end of the corridor, stopping before a carved wooden door half-open on rusted hinges. Inside, a writing desk sat beneath a dust-speckled window. Against the wall, an old raised platform, once used for prayer or meditation, waited in silence. This room had always been forbidden. Grandfather Udom called it Grandpa Thien's sanctuary.

The air inside was still, almost watchful. Shinakal stepped across the threshold as he reached up to open the second panel. A wooden box tumbled straight down and smacked the top of his head.

Thud!

"Ow…dammit, Grandpa!" he yelped, rubbing his scalp. "If you wanted me to find this, couldn't you just set it on the desk? No need to hurl it at me!"

He picked up the box and opened it. Inside were bundles of letters and a diary bound in animal hide. It didn't follow modern dates, more like a memoir written in hindsight.

Udom had once told him that "Shinakal" had been

Grandpa Thien's real name. He'd always thought it was just a family myth. But now… the evidence was in his hands.

"To Shinakal… From Phi Thep."

Curiosity bloomed. A man writing to another man and using his name? That was enough for Shinakal to shove the letters and diary into his canvas satchel. He scanned the room. There was nothing else of obvious value. Just old writing tools and antique furniture. He gently closed the door, ready to let the cleaners take over before the nobleman's visit the next day.

Chapter 10

"Shin!"

A voice called out from the front porch. Traditional Thai houses didn't come with doorbells, so anyone visiting had to yell. Shinakal quickly stuffed the diary he'd been reading halfway into a drawer and rushed to greet his visitor.

Phonphol had arrived, looking more formal than usual in a tailored jacket and slacks, accompanied by a client.

"This is **Mom Rajawongse Rapeekorn**," he introduced. "Department head at the Ministry of Culture. He's really interested in this house. As soon as I mentioned you were selling, he asked me to bring him over right away."

Mom Rapeekorn wore a designer shirt and tailored pants. If no one had introduced him as a member of a royal family,

Shinakal would have guessed he was a model or a startup CEO. With his clean-shaven face, strong eyebrows, large expressive eyes, and high-bridged nose, he had the sort of striking features that felt timeless, though his skin had a rich, golden undertone often seen in ancient Thai murals.

He offered his hand in a Western-style handshake. Shinakal, slightly flustered, shook it back.

"Good morning, Mom Rapeekorn," he began, unsure whether to use royal speech or not. But the nobleman read his nervousness with a quick smile.

"Please, just call me Rapee, like Phonphol does. I don't cling to formalities. No need for royal speak."

"Alright then… I'll just call you 'Mom.' Calling you by name feels strange. I'm afraid I'll get mouth ulcers from the guilt," Shinakal joked, trying to lighten the mood.

Strangely, even though Mom Rapeekorn hadn't bought the place yet, he already seemed perfectly at home. He moved through the rooms as if he owned them, and even his scent matched the floral fragrance drifting in from the garden. It was uncanny.

"So why are you selling this house, Mr. Shin?" Mom Rapeekorn asked, his eyes traveling carefully over the room, examining every detail with calm, deliberate elegance. Shinakal couldn't help but be a little impressed. Maybe all the noble-born were taught to carry themselves that way.

"The economy tanked," Shinakal replied with a sigh. "I have to keep my café afloat. If I don't, I'll have to start laying off staff. Selling this house is the only way."

"Do you know the history of this house?" Mom Rapeekorn asked, though it didn't sound like a question.

Shinakal shook his head.

"This house was a gift from Prince Khun Luang to your great-great-grandfather, who was one of his Khon performers."

"What, really? A prince giving a house like this to a performer? That's some serious affection."

Shinakal glanced around. The house was big, yes, but by modern standards it wasn't a mansion. Still, a gift like this wasn't given lightly. The performer must have been someone special.

"In the old days, close servants of the royal family were

rarely commoners," Mom Rapeekorn explained. "Some were minor nobles, even childhood friends of royalty. It wasn't unusual, even in other countries, for kings to gift land or property to loyal bodyguards or companions who had risked their lives for them. For someone of real influence, a house like this was just a token."

His voice was calm and deep, but carried a persuasive charm. Even someone like Shinakal, who had nearly flunked history, found himself nodding along. Meanwhile, Phonphol had slipped away mid-conversation to take a call. He returned, rubbing his stomach and complaining. "Let's go eat. Shin's buying."

"You drag me along just to pay the bill?" Shinakal shot back, trying to keep it light even as irritation crept into his voice. He clamped his mouth shut before saying more. There's no point in picking a fight in front of the customer. If the deal went through, Phonphol would walk away with a million-baht commission, yet here he was pinching pennies over lunch. Typical business with friends. Shinakal let out a sharp exhale.

***

"One iced milk tea, please," said a familiar voice.

Shinakal looked up from the high bar table in his café. It was meant for customers to sip coffee, but he usually used it to calculate monthly expenses.

"Mom Rapeekorn," he greeted, using the man's full title despite being told not to. "How did you know I was running a café here?"

"Phon told me," Mom Rapeekorn replied with a sly grin. "I have my spies around you, too."

Shinakal could tell he was joking, but strangely, the mention of spies made him think of his great-grandfather's old diary.

"There's nothing interesting about me that anyone would need to send a spy for," Shinakal shot back.

"Oh, but that's where you're wrong. You're very interesting."

Shinakal blinked, caught off guard. Was he hearing things, or did the prince flirt with him?

"Don't say that. I might actually believe it," he said with

a small, uneasy laugh.

He'd never announced he liked men, but he'd never tried to hide it either. He was comfortable with who he was, and his family hadn't made a fuss. The only thing he'd never tried was dressing like a woman.

"I wasn't joking," Mom Rapeekorn replied, his smile disarmingly genuine.

Seriously, Shinakal! Focus. Business first. You have a house to sell!

"Mr. Rapeekorn, your iced tea is ready!" called his barista, rescuing Shinakal from the intense moment.

The nobleman walked over to get his drink and sat back beside Shinakal again. The café owner swallowed. Watching the client's jaw work the straw felt dangerously distracting. He forced himself to look away before changing the topic.

"So… what brings you here today?" he asked, trying to sound casual.

"I'm looking for someone to go see the Khon performance with me at Sala Chalermkrung."

Shinakal raised an eyebrow. With his modern face and ripped jeans, he was probably the last person anyone would think to invite to a traditional masked drama.

"I… don't know if I'll understand it," he admitted. He didn't even know the characters in the Ramakien, so how was he supposed to follow the plot?

"Khon isn't just about following a story. It's movement. Rhythm. Pure expression. Think of it like watching a martial arts film, except it's set in Thailand and is elegant. The swordplay is basically choreography."

"Honestly? I don't even like kung fu movies. But… sure. I'll give it a shot. Might be… educational." He slung his messenger bag over his shoulder, trying to act casual.

"Do we need tickets or anything?"

"Handled. My friend's performing tonight. He's Canadian, actually. Came here to study Khon. Even performed in front of royalty."

"A Canadian? Doing Khon?" Shinakal's jaw dropped. He felt heat crawl up his neck. "I'm Thai and I've never even seen it live…"

"Did you know your great-great-grandfather was a Khon performer?" Mom Rapeekorn remarked with an arched brow. Of course, Shinakal knew. Mom Rapeekorn told him that back at the old Thai house.

Shinakal let out an exaggerated huff and folded his arms in mock indignation. "Oh yeah? You wanna take this outside or wrestle here in the café?"

Mom Rapeekorn's laugh was low and easy, the sound of someone who never really lost his composure. "Come now, don't be dramatic. I'm only teasing. You just looked so endearingly flustered, that's all." He glanced around the café with an air of mild amusement before returning his calm gaze to Shinakal. "Truth is, Khon used to be taught only in the royal court, mostly to the children of the nobility. By the reign of King Rama III, it was nearly lost altogether. So I can't fault anyone for not knowing much about it now."

"Why did the king try to abolish it?"

"Because people in the palace used to spend every day watching Khon instead of working. It was like how our neighbors throw parties every weekend. The king got tired of it. He told everyone to get real jobs that benefited the country. That's why Bangkok thrived during his reign. He was a savvy merchant king. Even King Rama II called him a Jao Sua (Business Tycoon)."

Mom Rapeekorn recited the history like someone who had actually lived through it. It was weirdly charming.

"If you said you were a history teacher, I'd believe you," Shinakal said as they reached the prince's car.

Mom Rapeekorn opened the passenger door for him.

No one had ever done that for Shinakal before. Did he dress that femininely today?

"Do you believe in reincarnation?" Mom Rapeekorn asked suddenly after sliding into the driver's seat.

"Um… like those soap operas where people remember past lives?" Shinakal wasn't sure where this conversation was heading - superstition, karma, or perhaps some body-swap fantasy. Instead of answering, Mom Rapeekorn just smiled and turned the ignition, leaving the question hanging in the air.

What a weirdo! Shinakal shot him a side glance. If

Phonpol hadn't confirmed this guy was real royalty, he might've bailed out of the car by now.

The European car cruised for a while before arriving at the theater that used to be the famous Sala Chalermkrung cinema. Shinakal hadn't been in this part of town for ages. Now it was all tuk-tuks and tour buses clogging the road.

Mom Rapeekorn led him backstage to meet Khun Benjamin, a khon performer with a Western face but a body smaller than most Thais. Shinakal embarrassed himself immediately when the prince introduced the foreigner as a "monkey."

"You play Hanuman?" Shinakal asked, eyeing the intricate white monkey costume that left only Benjamin's head visible.

"Nope," Benjamin said with a quick shake of the head.

"What? But didn't you say you play a monkey?" Now Benjamin chuckled.

"Oh, there are lots of monkeys in the Ramakien," he said.

Oof. Pecked by my own chicken again, Shinakal thought. How could a foreigner beat him at being Thai? Thankfully, Benjamin didn't seem to mind. The good-humored actor even listed the names of the different monkey characters for him. None of which Shinakal could remember, of course. It's a good thing this wasn't an exam.

"Are you into khon, Mom Rapeekorn? Is that why you want to buy my great-grandfather's house?" Shinakal asked, trying to steer the conversation elsewhere while waiting for the show.

"No."

"Then… you want to preserve old architecture?" Shinakal tried again.

Mom Rapeekorn shook his head, that calm, princely composure making Shinakal grit his teeth. He was like Henry Cavill with a royal accent, irritatingly perfect, effortlessly charming. How did anyone even pull that off?

Shinakal just kept looking at him, refusing to drop the question. Finally, Mom Rapeekorn sighed, that steady, unflappable calm never wavering. When he spoke, his voice was low but perfectly honest.

"I'm looking for a treasure," he said.

***

"If there was any treasure in Grandpa Thien's house, Dad'd have dug it up and sold it years ago," Shinakal said dryly over the phone. He thumbed through the old diary anyway, eyes scanning for any hint of a hidden map, but there was nothing.

The truth was simple and ugly: they were selling the place because no one could afford to keep it up anymore. An old wooden house in the heart of Bangkok sounded romantic, until you saw the termites and the bills. Better to let it go than watch it rot.

"You think he meant, like, some treasure of the heart crap?" Phonpol drawled.

"Beats me. But seriously… don't you think Mom Rapeekorn's a little weird?

"Define weird."

"I dunno," Shinakal scratched at his hair, feeling stupid even saying it. "He's got this vibe like he's some prince from the past who time-traveled here to mess with us."

"Go to bed, man. You've been watching too many fantasy dramas." Shinakal could practically hear Phonpol rolling his eyes on the other end.

"Go to bed?" Shinakal narrowed his brows. "Why are you trying so hard to get me off the phone? You heading somewhere?"

"Yeah, and I don't have to report it to you. You're not my boyfriend," Phonpol shot back. He was probably the only person who knew Shinakal liked men, but their friendship had never once gotten weird because of it—total comfort, no bedroom confusion, ever.

"I'm your friend. I have the right to be nosy."

"Promise you won't laugh before I tell you," Phonpol warned. But Shinakal didn't even let him finish; he was already cracking up.

"See? This is exactly why I didn't want to tell you!"

"I'm getting it out of my system now so I won't laugh later. Spill!"

"You gonna listen or not?" Phonpol sighed, clearly regretting everything.

"No oath needed. I know you'd fry if you made one. Just talk."

"···Okay, so there's this tomboy girl, right? Her dad's forcing her to get married. She and I used to know each other, so she hired me to pretend to be her boyfriend to impress her dad…"

"You mean you got a gig as a man-whore," Shinakal cut in.

"Damn it! Could you at least say it in a way that sounds respectable?"

"You're being paid to act like her man. What else do you call it?" Shinakal laughed again. Maybe a bit too much.

"I'm helping an old friend, okay? Be nice and wipe that dog off your voice!"

The laughter only grew louder, and even tears started

streaming down his face. This was pure gossip gold.

"Seriously? How long have you known her? You never mentioned anything."

"You know her too. It's Saipan. I used to date her, remember?"

Shinakal furrowed his brow, digging through dusty memories until he pictured a cute, top-bun girl they'd gone to school with. They'd been together for a while, though to this day, he wasn't sure why they split.

"Saipan's a tomboy?"

"Yeah."

"She turned into a tomboy after breaking up with you?" This time, Shinakal really lost it. Surely, if he'd sworn not to laugh, he'd have been struck by lightning by now.

"I'm done talking to you. Take a dump or something. I'm hanging up," Phonpol growled, actually sounding mad.

"Wait! Are you meeting her tonight?" Shinakal clung to the conversation. For some reason, he didn't want to be home alone.

"Yeah… you wanna come?" Phonpol sighed. Truth be told, he'd feel better with backup. It had been ages since he saw Saipan. Last time they parted, it was ugly. She humiliated him in front of a whole party, and the entire school knew he'd been dumped.

Was this meeting a setup for revenge?

"Of course I'm coming! I wouldn't miss this for the rest world."

***

They cleaned up and got dressed before heading to a pulsing pub on Ratchadaphisek Road. Saipan had given simple instructions: "Just tell the bouncer you're here for me." They assumed she'd booked a table. Turned out, she owned the whole damn place.

Inside, the music throbbed, and neon lights cast vivid colors over sleek, glass-topped tables. Waitstaff in coordinated black bustled around, and the crowd looked effortlessly cool. When they gave her name at the door, a bouncer politely led them through the packed floor to a prime VIP section with a sweeping view of the stage.

Saipan spotted them first. She strode over and smacked Phonpol's shoulder with a grin that was pure trouble.

"Hey! Long time no see."

She was impossible to miss. Clad in a sheer black suit jacket over a crisp white button-down, tailored perfectly to her lean frame, the look was androgynous but undeniably stylish. Her hair fell in a sleek, straight curtain down her back, with bold silver-highlighted bangs that caught the light every time she moved.

Phonpol went stiff as a board. He used to be hopeless over that sweet, mischievous face. Even now, with her tomboy swagger and nightclub-boss aura. Some traitorous part of him wanted to just…hug her. And that, right there, was the exact reason he'd taken this crazy "job" in the first place. Even knowing how badly it might blow up in his face.

Chapter 11

Shinakal was jolted awake by a relentless series of ding! Ding! Ding! That seemed to pierce straight through his skull. He groaned, blindly fumbling for his phone on the nightstand, hoping it was something urgent enough to justify ruining his sleep.

But the moment the screen lit up, his stomach sank. It was a photo of him. Dead asleep, face tucked scandalously into Mom Rapeekorn's chest like he belonged there.

"What the…"

He sat up too quickly and instantly regretted it as the room lurched sideways. His head throbbed, nausea pooled in his gut, and he pressed a palm to his forehead like it could keep his brain from splitting in half.

As if that weren't enough, his phone buzzed again, this

time a call. Same sender. Clearly eager to enjoy his horror in real-time.

"How did anyone even get a picture of me… doing that?" he mumbled, voice raw with disbelief. There was no denying it. He let out a frustrated sigh and flopped back onto the pillow, dragging it over his head to block out the mocking daylight.

The whole mess began when Shinakal discovered that Saipan was actually Mom Rapeekorn's cousin; his father was her mother's brother. As if that wasn't enough, they'd all ended up at her birthday party, where she introduced her "fake boyfriend," Phonpol. One thing led to another. The whole group got far too friendly and drank far too much. By the end of the night, Shinakal genuinely couldn't remember who had even managed to drag him home.

"So did Mom Rapeekorn go home yet?"

"What?" Shinakal shot upright in bed, eyes wide. Home? Don't tell me he actually stayed over. He didn't have long to panic. A knock rattled the bedroom door, and the warm, savory smell of bacon drifting in through the gap was all the answer he needed.

"Are you awake enough for breakfast?" came that calm, smooth voice, the same one that must have driven his drunk self home last night.

"Yeah! I'm up!" He scrambled out of bed in a fluster, checking frantically to make sure he at least had his underwear on. He'd woken up drunk at home before, but never with the added worry that actual nobility might have seen his bare ass.

No time for a shower. He wrestled himself into a pair of shorts, hair sticking up like a startled cat. Toothbrush in mouth, he squeezed half the tube onto the bristles, scrubbed with frantic determination, spit, rinsed, and sprinted for the table. He tried to stroll in like nothing was unusual, but it was a hopeless, spectacular failure.

"Why didn't you wake me up sooner?" he asked, glancing at the clock. Nearly noon. Bacon and an omelet sat on toast. Basically, brunch at this point. Mom Rapeekorn looked completely unbothered.

"Older folks wake up early. You're young. Sleeping in is allowed."

Older folks? He was only like ten years older! Not exactly ancient.

"Look, just tell me if I did anything humiliating last night. Go on. Ruin me now so I know if I need to grovel and give up on selling you the house, or if I can still take you to sign the contract." His mouth really didn't have a filter. At least Mom Rapeekorn just chuckled softly.

"Don't worry about it. No one blames drunk people."

"Maybe you don't. I do. Did I do anything…handsy?"

"Do you normally get handsy with people when you're drunk?" Mom Rapeekorn arched a brow. He cracked his egg with practiced finesse, salt and chili flakes scattering perfectly over the broken yolk. British-style, he called it, to avoid a mess. But Shinakal couldn't handle chili with eggs. Too spicy for him.

"At least no one's gotten pregnant so far," Shinakal deadpanned. "Last I checked, no doctors are willing to install ovaries in men."

So much for subtlety, guess he might as well admit he was into men, since he'd already passed out on Mom Rapeekorn's chest. And if the guy didn't leave soon? Hell, he'd do more than cling. He'd grab his waist, his thigh, maybe even grind like they were at a salsa club. Because now? He was sober and all too aware of it.

"So… did I get handsy with you or not?"

"Define 'handsy'." Mom Rapeekorn's smile was positively devilish.

Shinakal froze, fork halfway to his mouth. He watched Mom Rapeekorn watching him, then the older man actually set his own fork down, surrendering like a knight laying down his sword.

Please. Do whatever you want. I'm love's prisoner. Hopelessly bound by love. Hurt me, hold me, haunt me—just don't let go.

"Words don't quite do it justice. Let me show you instead." The young man lifted the toast halfway to his mouth, then stopped, because eating would ruin the drama of the moment.

A gentle laugh rumbled in her throat. Calm and elegant as ever, Mom Rapeekorn gave a slow nod.

Permission granted.

Shinakal nudged his half-eaten sandwich aside and rose from his chair, the scrape of wood barely audible. He moved without a word, with no buildup or warning. Just the sudden lean-in, the press of lips catching Mom Rapeekorn mid-breath. His mouth was impossibly soft, like brushed velvet. No bristle met her skin, just smooth warmth and a faint scent of mint—impeccable grooming, despite the night spent elsewhere. When Shinakal pulled back, his tongue flicked over Mom Rapeekorn's lips, slow and deliberate, as if savoring whatever lingered.

"That's what I call handsy," Sinkal murmured, voice thick as dusk.

Mom Rapeekorn didn't even blink. He murmured, "Feels like last night you did more than that."

"Can you…define 'more'?" Shinakal blinked. That earned him a slow, wicked smile.

Mom Rapeekorn stood up smoothly, peeling off the T-shirt he'd borrowed last night. His hair sprang back into shape, model-perfect. He looked like he'd just walked off a bad-boy fashion spread. He ran his fingers through Shinakal's hair, stopping at the back of his neck. The touch was possessive as he tipped his head back with quiet command. He didn't go for the mouth right away. Instead, he planted slow kisses along his jaw, then whispered against his ear.

"Did you know that back in your great-grandfather's day, Thais didn't even kiss?"

"Then what did they do?" Shinakal managed, eyes fluttering shut until he felt himself shoved against the wall.

"They pressed cheeks. Like this."

He demonstrated by grazing Shinakal's cheek with his lips while his other hand pressed firmly against the bulge in Shinakal's shorts.

"And they teased each other."

Mom Rapeekorn's fingers hooked in the waistband, tugging it down. Impatient, Shinakal just yanked them off himself, sticking out his tongue and leaning in like he demanded another kiss.

"Teasing is cruel, Mom," he panted. "Don't hold out on me."

Mom Rapeekorn chuckled low in his throat. "Back then, people chewed betel nut. Their mouths would be stained bright red. Not exactly sexy to kiss."

Shinakal barked out a laugh, then immediately buried his face in Mom Rapeekorn's chest. "Lucky I wasn't born in that era."

"Do you believe in reincarnation?" Mom Rapeekorn's eyes softened, fingers stroking his hair

"Is this a real question, or a line? Can we talk about it after I ravish you?" Shinakal snorted. Mom Rapeekorn pinched his ass hard enough to make him yelp.

"Ow! Why the hell did you do that?"

"You're too tempting." Mom Rapeekorn's gaze dropped from Shinakal's mouth to the rest of his body, taking in the fact that Shinakal was now completely naked.

Shinakal crossed his arms, suddenly aware of the unfairness.

"Okay, your shirt. Off. Now."

Mom Rapeekorn raised a brow but didn't move.

"Can't," he said with infuriating calm. "I have lunch with my aunt. Saipan's mom."

Shinakal's face twisted. "What? You can't just roll up with your cannon aimed at my city gates and then turn your army around back to Burma!"

Mom Rapeekorn let out a slow laugh at the melodrama.

"I need to change first or I'll be late. Unless you want to come along?"

"Come as what? Your date? Hard pass," Shinakal grumbled, stepping away to scoop up his clothes. He'd have to finish this in the bathroom—solo. Mom Rapeekorn tilted his head, smiling indulgently.

"I promise I'll come back and finish the siege tonight."

"Yeah, fine. Whatever." Shinakal let out a suffering sigh. He bit into his sandwich, practically swallowing half of it in one chomp. The other half he carried into the bathroom, refusing to say goodbye. He couldn't help sulking.

Seriously? They'd spent the whole damn night in the same house and a full morning together. And somehow, he still hadn't managed to get Mom Rapeekorn into bed. He hadn't been "deflowered" so much as… well. Let's say his flowers had been thoroughly plucked already—front door, back door, hell, if his sides had doors they'd be gone too. But apparently? Mom Rapeekorn was still perfectly intact, aggravatingly so.

***

Shinakal had never sat around waiting for an older man to come over before. And yet here he was—pacing around his room like some lovesick teen, checking the clock every three minutes and pretending not to care. Not that Mom Rapeekorn was that old. The man didn't even limp—no signs of osteoporosis. Definitely didn't need a cane. Still, Shinakal felt ridiculous. Restless. A little too aware of how soft his own lips probably looked.

"Oh my god, get a grip," he muttered to himself, running both hands through his already-messy hair. "You're not starring in a BL drama."

He needed to do something. Anything. Before he lost his mind. Or worse—spiraled into full-blown horny panic.

Finally, he couldn't take it anymore. Snatching up his keys, he stormed out of the house and drove straight to his great-grandfather's place.

Because that made total sense. Right?

Right.

Actually, he was hooked on that old diary. It read like a melodramatic romance novel—complete with mystery, villains, heroes, and a loyal sidekick. He was dying to see what happened next. But the second he pulled up, his heart sank. The front door was busted open, hinges hanging loose.

Son of a bitch. Those antique doors were impossible to replace. Some asshole had pried it apart for fun. He ran straight for the study. The door was ajar. The desk was overturned. Papers were everywhere—the old letters and the diary were scattered all over the floor.

Thank God the thief hadn't bothered to steal them. He scrambled to gather everything, praying none of it was too severely damaged. Then he froze.

Something cold pressed against his throat.

"Where's the enameled pendant?" a low voice hissed in his ear.

Shinakal's heart pounded. The guy hadn't fled. He'd hidden behind the door, waiting for someone to come in.

"Pendant? What pendant?" he asked, faking dumb.

He vaguely remembered seeing that word in the diary, but he'd never actually seen any jewel or photo of it. The cold point twitched at his neck, then suddenly yanked away.

Someone else had grabbed the thief from behind.

"Aaagh!"

Shinakal didn't wait to see what happened. He bolted to the side, clutching the papers. Out of the corner of his eye, he saw Mom Rapeekorn slamming his knee into the mugger's ribs, throwing him backward like something out of a damn movie.

Holy shit, the old man's a badass. Where the hell did he get that strength? Even he couldn't knee someone into the air like that.

"Watch out, behind you!" Shinakal shouted as another thug lunged in.

Mom Rapeekorn ducked smoothly, the knife swiping harmlessly over his head.

"OMG!" Shinakal gasped. "You're like a kung fu movie!"

Mom Rapeekorn didn't answer. He twisted the first guy's arm until there was a sickening crack, wrested the knife away, and turned to face the second. But that one wasn't stupid. He just grabbed his wounded friend and ran. Mom Rapeekorn didn't bother chasing them. He turned to Shinakal, eyes scanning for injuries.

"Are you alright?" His voice was low and tense. Shinakal took a shaky breath. Then glared.

"How the hell did you know I was here? That's twice now.

Are you stalking me or something?" His heart was still hammering, and he hated how weird this all felt.

Shinakal edged away carefully, hugging the rescued papers. He'd been sitting at home all morning waiting for Mom Rapeekorn, finally got sick of it, and came here instead, planning to read the diary in peace. Instead, he got burglars. And apparently… a personal bodyguard with psychic timing.

"I'm not a stalker," Mom Rapeekorn said calmly. He was still holding the mugger's knife, which made Shinakal eye it warily.

Mom Rapeekorn dropped to one knee, set the knife on the floor, and nudged it over with his foot. Shinakal snatched it up and held it tight. He wasn't sure he trusted him yet. Not because he thought Mom Rapeekorn would stab him… but because this was too weird.

His house wasn't even close to Mom Rapeekorn's place. He wouldn't just run into him here by accident.

"You're lying," Shinakal snapped. "You had to come here on purpose. Why? Waiting to ambush me?"

"I'm not a stalker. I saw it. I knew you'd be attacked today." Mom Rapeekorn raised his hands in surrender.

Shinakal blinked. *What.* He squinted at the other man like he was insane. "Excuse me?"

Mom Rapeekorn's voice stayed calm, but there was urgency in it.

"After I met with Saipan's mom, I drove straight here. I

knew they'd be waiting. I wanted to warn you. But I realized if I tried, you wouldn't believe me. So I came to stop them instead." He spread his hands again, palms up, showing he had no other weapons.

"And… I know what's in the diary you're holding. I keep asking you if you believe in reincarnation because… you are Thien. Your great-grandfather. Reborn."

Chapter 12

Things surrounding the mystery of the bridal house were getting messier by the day. Shinakal couldn't hold it in anymore. He had to call someone to vent his frustrations. Unfortunately, the person on the other end turned into Sherlock Holmes mid-conversation.

"So let me get this straight," Phonpol said, summarizing his wild theory. "Mom Rapeekorn wants to buy the house and cozy up to you because he's after Great-Grandpa Thien's pendant. He had read those diaries before, which is how he knew they belonged to your great-grandfather. And maybe he even sent those thugs to rob you in the first place so that he could show up and play hero."

Phonpol didn't actually believe Mom Rapeekorn had

psychic powers or access to past lives. It was just too far out for science. But in a world where anything might be possible, this was the most logical explanation he could come up with. The whole thing was so convoluted that Shinakal's poor little brain couldn't keep up. He got up from bed and slumped into the chair at his desk, massaging his temples.

"Why the hell would those thieves want the pendant so badly?" he muttered, scribbling a question mark onto a notepad. Sure, it was gold. But a little enamelled jewellery wasn't worth that much. Wouldn't it be easier to yank a necklace off some wealthy socialite? Why tear apart an old house just for a single antique?

And what about Mom Rapeekorn? He really wanted to buy the place to search for Great-Grandpa Thien's pendant! Was that pendant seriously worth more than the house itself?

It didn't add up. Borderline absurd. The price Mom Rapeekorn had offered for the house was way over market value. What the hell was he thinking?

The answer, Shinakal suspected, had to be buried in Great-Grandpa Thien's secret diary.

Khon Spy Behind the Fallen Prince

***

Shinakal had stayed up all night reading the diary until he finally passed out. His alarm blared early in the morning. He had promised to go on a trip out of town with Phonpol, who insisted Shinakal tag along as his third-wheel backup.

"I'm gay, in case you forgot," Shinakal reminded him pointedly when Phonpol asked him to help cockblock a straight girl who was obsessed with his fake girlfriend, the LGBTQ girlfriend.

"I know! I'm the only straight guy in the group. But that lesbian girl just won't stop flirting with Saipan! I've tried everything. Every time I take Saipan out, I end up third-wheeling my own date."

The "lesbian girl" in question was Wanlapa, a stunning model with long hair, a tiny waist, and outrageously large boobs—not that Shinakal wanted to look, but the damn things looked like they were about to fall out of her shirt. It was hard not to notice.

He'd met her once at Saipan's birthday party, held at a pub. She was practically glued to Saipan the whole night.

207

"I thought you were just a fake boyfriend?" Shinakal asked.

That was all it took. Phonpol immediately scooted closer, despite the fact that no one was around to eavesdrop.

"Remember the night we ran into Uncle Phichitchai at Saipan's party?"

"You mean the night of 'the fake boyfriend' was introduced to her family?" Shinakal nodded.

"Well, turns out Uncle Phichitchai cornered me in the bathroom that night. Wanted to talk. In the bathroom. Weird as hell." Phonpol had a way of telling stories that made his life sound way more dramatic than anyone else's, and with his looks, he could outshine most runway models to begin with.

"Just get to the point."

"Okay, bottom line? Her dad totally saw through us. He said our fake dating stunt was straight out of a bad soap opera and anyone who still falls for it is a moron."

Shinakal burst out laughing.

"So now," Phonpol continued, "the dad who figured it all out wants to hire me, pay me double, to actually turn Saipan into my real girlfriend. Like curing the tomboy and making her the mother of his grandchildren. If she agrees, he'll give me half the company."

"Holy shit. That's worse than before!" Shinakal wasn't even joking. The whole thing screamed of bribery and generational madness.

"Who you yelling at?"

"You, you asshole. Loud and clear enough for you?"

"Alright, alright! I get it. I'm the worst. Can we move on?" Phonpol grinned before softening his voice with a sigh. "Look, I know I'm a bastard. But I really do love Saipan. When I first agreed to play the fake boyfriend, it was because I wanted a shot at her. I was scared her dad would find out. But now? Her dad's practically greenlit the mission! If I back out now, I won't just be a jerk. I'll be an idiot. Double loser. Walking L. Might as well wear a sign that says 'kick me.'"

This time, Shinakal didn't know what to say. Part of him wanted to smack his friend, but the other part genuinely pitied him. Life was weird. Of all the girls in Thailand, Phonpol had to fall for Saipan, and he'd been hung up on her since high school.

"I also did warn Uncle Phichitchai," Phonpol said. "Told him it wouldn't work. But he said, 'We used to be together before. If anyone can turn her around, it's you. You know her best.'"

"So now you've got hope."

"Hell yeah, I've got hope. With a future father-in-law like that? My only problem now is how to get Wanlapa out of the picture. That's why I need you. I saw the way she looked at you the other night."

"Don't drag me into this. I don't even remember what I did that night. For all we know, she was staring at me because I looked like a lunatic." A lunatic who got drunk, danced on stage with the DJ, and kissed a literal royal, Mom Rapeekorn, on the mouth…

Just thinking about that night made Shinakal groan. He hadn't dared face Mom Rapeekorn since. The guy might be ridiculously hot, but if he turned out to be a rich stalker, Shinakal was out. So when Phonpol invited him on this trip, he jumped at the chance. Anything to get his mind off the mysterious prince.

Their plan was first to drive out to the floating market for noodles. Then head to Uncle Phichitchai's vacation home in Phetchaburi. This trip wasn't random. It was part of the father-in-law's master plan. Saipan agreed to come only because her dad let Wanlapa tag along. Meanwhile, her girlfriend had been begging to visit the house for ages. The dad claimed it was too far to send just the girls alone, so they needed a male chaperone. Which meant this van now carried three LGBTQ+ folks and one desperate straight guy trying to make a tomboy fake girlfriend his baby mama. It was still unclear who would change who or who would break who, but things weren't looking great for the lone straight man.

After Phonpol mentioned Wanlapa's stares, Shinakal started paying attention. And he had to admit, his friend was right. Wanlapa was watching him. But not in a flirty way. More like… sidelong glances. Secretive. Hard to read. And Phonpol wasn't exaggerating about not being able to separate the girls either. Saipan and Wanlapa were practically joined at the hip, literally. If Saipan wasn't holding her hand, Wanlapa was clinging to her arm. They alternated with the ease of tentacles. Not to mention all the cheek-kissing and head-nuzzling going on in the back seat.

Like the world only had room for the two of them.

If Shinakal didn't know them, he'd assume they were trying to seduce Phonpol into a threesome. And honestly, maybe they were. Since every time the girls got handsy, Phonpol's pants got tighter. The poor guy had to keep shifting in his seat just to hide the evidence.

"Dude, chill out. Your face looks like you just swallowed wasabi."

"You finally get how much I'm suffering, huh?" Phonpol's voice cracked with desperation. Shinakal nodded furiously, though he had no clue how to help.

When the van stopped for gas, he did the only thing he could think of: he rushed to the restroom, then stocked up on snacks and drinks like he was preparing for a siege. On his way back to the van, he spotted Wanlapa standing in the shadowy corner near the building. At first, he thought she was chatting with Saipan, but when he reached the van, Saipan was already inside, chatting with Phonpol.

So… who the hell was Wanlapa talking to?

Curious, Shinakal stepped back and decided to spy a little.

And that's when he saw him.

"Mom Rapeekorn?" he gasped. The man standing in the corner looked just like him. But when Shinakal tried to get a closer look, the figure slipped behind the building.

"Who was that?" he asked, pretending not to know.

"Just… someone asking for directions," she said quickly, a little too quickly. Her face had gone pale.

"Wasn't that Mom Rapeekorn?" he pressed.

Of course, she knew who he meant. Mom Rapeekorn was Saipan's cousin. They'd met at her birthday party.

"It wasn't. If it were him, he'd have said hi to Saipan," she said breezily, then brushed past him and headed for the van. Shinakal didn't push further. After all, if it had been Mom Rapeekorn… why would he run away? Unless he was still embarrassed from being called a stalker the other day!

***

The van arrived at Uncle Phichitchai's beachfront vacation home just before sunset. After a quick dinner at a seaside restaurant, the group settled into their rooms. No one had the energy for anything else after such a long drive. Luckily, the villa was enormous. Everyone got their own room with a sea view, just steps away from a beach lined with famous restaurants and luxury hotels.

Shinakal woke earlier than anyone else. He hadn't slept well. He'd spent half the night staring at his phone. Mom Rapeekorn still hadn't texted. Not even a cheeky message about buying the house, like usual.

He wanted to stay mad, but part of him worried that staying mad too long would make him lose the sale. By evening, he figured he'd swallow his pride and shoot the guy a quick apology for blowing up at him the other night. Then fate happened.

Out for a morning walk along the beach, Shinakal found himself face-to-face with none other than…

"Mom?" he muttered, already feeling the annoyance bubble up again. Seriously? He'd come all the way to Phetchaburi, and the stalker prince still managed to show up?

No way he was letting this one slide.

"Well, well… didn't expect to see you here, Mr.

Shinakal," Mom Rapeekorn said smoothly, sipping coffee at a hotel restaurant like he belonged there.

"Don't play dumb. What do you want from me? Why are you following me again?" Shinakal stormed over and sat down across from him like a man on a mission.

Mom Rapeekorn raised a brow but said nothing. Before he could reply, a woman's voice cut in.

"Who's following who, dear?"

Shinakal froze. That voice was familiar. He turned just in time to see Pavannarath, a famous TV news host, approaching the table with a breakfast plate in hand. She sat down beside Mom Rapeekorn like it was the most normal thing in the world. Shinakal's eyebrows shot up twice as high as Mom's.

"This is Shinakal," Mom Rapeekorn introduced politely. "He owns the heritage Thai house I've been thinking of purchasing." Then he turned to the woman. "This is Pavannarath. She's hosting the seminar I'm speaking at today." He gestured casually toward the hotel's announcement board.

Wait—what? There was a seminar? Shinakal whipped his head around. Sure enough, a giant sign near the door read:

"Soft Power and Thai Culture – Guest Speaker: Mom Rapeekorn"

Oh god. He hadn't even noticed when he walked in. Must've been too blinded by rage to read signs.

"You're here for work?" he croaked. His rage started shriveling into sheer embarrassment.

"I… I'm so sorry," he stammered. "I didn't know you were here with… Ms. Pavannarath."

He shot to his feet and clasped his hands together, begging for forgiveness from the ghost of karma past.

He wanted to die. Or better yet, sink into the sand like a mythical Khmer mud demon and disappear forever.

"If you're not in a rush, why not join us for breakfast?" Mom Rapeekornsaid with a smile, raising a hand to summon the waiter.

Before Shinakal could protest, a flurry of hotel staff had swooped in. Three chairs appeared as if conjured by magic. Dishes and glasses were set before him with flawless precision. That's five-star service for you. No chance to escape, even if you wanted to.

"So you're the owner of that beautiful traditional house?" Pavannarath said warmly. "It's lovely. Mom showed me pictures. I wanted it myself, but he's already claimed it."

Claimed it?! Since when?! Shinakal wanted to ask, but biting his tongue seemed the safer route. He was already humiliated enough for one morning. So instead of opening his mouth again, he reached for the glass of water in front of him and took a long, deliberate sip.

If he didn't talk, he couldn't embarrass himself any further. That was the hope, anyway.

Mom Rapeekorn glanced at him over the rim of his coffee cup with a smirk that said I saw that.

As for Shinakal? He could almost hear the sound of chickens, his dignity, flapping off into the distance, never to return.

Chapter 13

"There you are, Shin! Where the hell have you been? We looked everywhere for you!" Phonpol griped the moment Shinakal stepped through the door.

He claimed he'd gone out to grab coffee. But the truth? He'd just let an entire chicken coop loose… and spent the rest of the morning trying to herd his pride back into its pen. Humiliated beyond belief, he nearly fled back to Bangkok. But guilt held him back. So instead, he stuck around and ended up walking Mom Rapeekorn to his seminar room, making small talk until he could finally slip away.

Not long after, his phone buzzed. It was a text from Mom Rapeekorn. He wanted to talk to Saipan, but her phone was off.

"It's not off. The battery just died," Saipan said, holding

out her hand. "Can I borrow yours?"

Shinakal handed his phone over without a word and made a quick escape. No way was he sticking around to accidentally overhear anything. That bad habit needed to die. Ignorance really was bliss—remember that, Shin.

The call didn't last ten minutes. When Saipan returned his phone, Phonpol and Wanlapa were busy debating their afternoon plans. There were tons of places to visit in Phetchaburi, but ever since diving into his great-grandfather Thien's diary, Shinakal had developed an obsession with historical sites. So he proposed a trip to Khao Luang Cave, where King Rama V once commissioned a Buddha image in honor of King Rama IV.

If they got there before noon, they'd even catch the famous beam of sunlight streaming into the cave.

What he didn't expect was to find you-know-who standing right at the cave entrance, grinning like the sunrise itself. Shinakal groaned.

"I'm not saying a word this time." He zipped his lips shut with an exaggerated gesture. No more yelling "stalker!" in public. Lesson learned. Still, how was it even possible to bump into this guy everywhere?

"I'll admit it," Mom Rapeekorn leaned in and whispered. "This time I did follow you."

Aha! Knew it! Shinakal spun around, jaw dropping. So, to recap: Shinakal was now perilously close to falling for someone who had literally confessed to stalking him. And as for the break-in at his great-grandfather's house? Still a mystery. But the royal stalker? Still suspect number one.

"Saipan invited me to join since I was already in town for the seminar," Mom Rapeekorn said casually. "I figured I'd play tour guide."

He raised his phone and snapped a photo of Saipan and Phonpol kneeling before a Buddha statue, bathed in a soft beam of sunlight. Then he offered it to Shinakal.

Saipan had asked for the photo herself. She wanted proof to show her dad she was really out on a date with Phonpol. Seeing the image made Shinakal smile, despite himself.

"You're really good at photography," he commented.

"The camera was expensive," Mom Rapeekorn replied

modestly.

"Ah, so you're just showing off how rich you are, huh?" Shinakal's teasing tone made Mom Rapeekorn beam even wider.

"Are you still mad?"

"I've been over it. You just didn't call, so I never got to say."

"Work's been insane. With the seminar and ministry duties."

He worked in public relations at the Ministry of Culture, according to Phonpol. Shinakal hadn't paid attention at the time.

It was their turn to pay respects to the Buddha image. Phonpol offered to take a photo, but Shinakal waved him off. Still, Phonpol took the shot anyway, and they didn't stop him.

"I hope I sell that house for a fortune," Shinakal murmured, loud enough for a certain someone to hear.

"Aren't you afraid the buyer might run away?" came the calm voice from beside him. The buyer, it seemed, had no intention of running anywhere.

"Nah. If he does, I'll know he wasn't serious." Shinakal smirked. He bowed deeply to the Buddha, then moved on to pay respects to four more statues. Each is dedicated to one of the first four kings of the Chakri dynasty.

***

Phonpol's life was once again slipping into chaos, though he didn't seem to mind. Ever since Mom Rapeekorn appeared on this so-called casual getaway, Saipan had completely stopped playfully kissing Wanlapa on the head. She was clearly too worried that her cousin might report back to her father. The result was simple. All her sweet attention shifted to Phonpol, and he was basking in it like a cat in the sun.

"Mom, can't you stay a little longer with us?" Phonpol asked, grinning as he peeled shrimp for Saipan like the most loyal boyfriend on Earth.

After the cave visit, the group made a quick stop at the royal palace and wrapped up the day at a breezy beachside restaurant. As the sun dipped low and the salty air played with their hair, Phonpol seized his moment. He peeled shrimp with exaggerated care, determined to earn every bit of affection Saipan was willing to show. But Saipan wasn't about to look like a helpless princess. She picked up the peeled shrimp and dropped it onto Wanlapa's plate instead, insisting it was only fair. Wanlapa's long nails made peeling anything nearly impossible. Still, Phonpol refused to stop. Shrimp after shrimp, he pressed on. If playing the part of a fake boyfriend meant dedicating the night to crustacean duty, he was fully committed.

"Mom is probably swamped with work and has to go back to Bangkok, right?" Shinakal cut in, tone stiff. The last thing he wanted was his possible stalker sticking around. He'd come on this trip to forget about the noble, not keep bumping into him.

"I can stay."

"What?!" Shinakal and Saipan blurted in unison.

"I thought you were leaving tomorrow morning!" Saipan protested, visibly anxious that her charade might get exposed.

"Your father called when he heard I was here for the seminar," the prince said calmly. "Asked me to keep an eye on you. I agreed."

That wiped the smile right off Saipan's face. Her dad had

officially deployed a royal-grade spy.

"You'll be staying at the villa with us then?" Phonpol asked, practically glowing with joy.

Rapeekorn nodded. Phonpol looked like he was about to leap over the table and hug the man. Shinakal kicked his friend under the table. Get a grip, his eyes warned.

Once dinner wrapped up and they were back at the villa, Shinakal couldn't help but ask what had been bugging him since lunch.

"Is it normal for rich people to send spies to watch their daughters?"

Mom Rapeekorn looked puzzled for a second until Shinakal tilted his head toward Saipan, currently walking along the beach with Phonpol glued to her side like a shadow.

"Oh… not just the rich," Mom Rapeekorn replied, touching his nose in a way that made it look like he was shielding his mouth. "Back in the day, kings sent spies into royal courts all the time. I'm sure your great-grandfather Thien knew all about that."

"You've read the diary?" Shinakal demanded, jumping to his feet. His brows scrunched up in suspicion.

"I haven't read it. But I do know the previous owner of that house quite well."

"That's a lie," Shinakal snapped. "My great-grandfather died long before you were even born. Don't pull that reincarnation card again. I don't buy it."

"You think I'd buy a house without researching who lived in it?"

Mom Rapeekorn's calm gaze met his. Those eyes saw too much. Too deep. And it was true. He knew things. More than just dates and names from a file. Shinakal sat back down, heavy with the realization.

"What do you know about him?"

"He was a spy sent to infiltrate the Khon dance troupe under Prince Khun Luang."

That stopped Shinakal cold. He collapsed onto the bench, heart thudding. Mom Rapeekorn knew more than any diary ever told him.

"Did he… succeed?" Shinakal asked quietly.

He should have been proud. If Grandpa Thien had succeeded, that meant he'd lived long and left a legacy. But instead, Shinakal just felt a strange, sinking sorrow.

"I'm not sure," Mom Rapeekorn said gently. "Did he write about it in his diary?"

Before Shinakal could answer, Wanlapa came rushing out of the house.

"Shin, have you seen Saipan?"

"She's probably down by the beach," Mom Rapeekorn answered for Shinakal.

"Oh, right. Uh… Shin, can you come with me? I left something in Saipan's bag and can't find it." She leaned in close, whispering like they were just two girlfriends.

"It's a tampon."

Shinakal glanced awkwardly at Mom Rapeekorn, who politely pretended not to hear. Then he got up and followed Wanlapa, used to doing weird errands for women who didn't trust "real men." But once they were out of earshot, Wanlapa suddenly turned serious.

"Don't trust Mom Rapeekorn too easily."

Shinakal froze, eyes darting around for Phonpol. Then he locked eyes with Wanlapa, who was staring straight at him.

"Why?"

"He told you about his past lives, didn't he? About karmic debts and all that?"

Chills ran up Shinakal's arms. She'd hit the nail right on the head. Mom Rapeekorn's odd words, the knowing gaze… They turned off the path and walked toward the dark stretch of sand, far from where Saipan and Phonpol were strolling.

"What does it mean?"

"In every life, we carry debts—betrayals, heartbreak, revenge. If you believe in reincarnation, you have to believe your karmic enemies will come back to settle the score." She stopped there.

"That's all I can say, Shin. I can't tell you more." And with that, she turned back the way they came. Shinakal stood there, heart pounding. He thought of what Mom Rapeekorn once told him. "You are Thien, reborn."

Great Grandpa Thien had been a spy, a servant to a powerful lord. If he'd succeeded in his mission, then he'd also betrayed that very same lord. Was that what Mom Rapeekorn had tried to warn him about all along?

Chapter 14

"I'm going home," Shinakal muttered, stuffing clothes into his suitcase with the kind of fury usually reserved for packing up a broken heart. There wasn't much, but what should've taken five minutes had turned into a tug-of-war. Every time he tossed in a shirt, Phonpol pulled it right back out and hung it up like none of this was happening.

"Come on, man. You can't leave now. It's almost midnight," Phonpol said, blocking the wardrobe with his body like a human doorstop. His tone tried to be casual, but the worry crept through. If Shinakal left, Mom Rapeekorn would probably go too. Phonpol didn't fancy becoming the leftover wheel in Saipan's love triangle. Still, mostly, he just didn't want his best friend out on the road alone at this hour.

"I'll grab a cab. Phetchaburi to Bangkok, what, under three hours without traffic?" Shinakal snapped. His voice was small but sharp, like a blade wrapped in silk. He knew it wasn't Phonpol's fault, but he was mad at everyone. Mad at Mom Rapeekorn for chasing him endlessly with secrets too bizarre to ignore. Mad at Wanlapa for warning him to stay away. Mad at that damn tomboy who refused to love his best friend, wasting everyone's time. And mad at Phonpol, for falling for her in the first place. Of all the girls in the world, he had to fall for her. What a pain.

"I'll take you," said a calm voice from the doorway. Mom Rapeekorn had walked in quietly after overhearing the argument from his room nearby.

"I'd rather go alone," Shinakal refused, shaking his head and avoiding eye contact. Looking at Mom Rapeekorn made something twist in his chest.

Why him? Why did it have to be him? Every time their eyes met, his heart faltered. And when Mom Rapeekorn was kind, Shinakal couldn't tell if it was genuine or part of some elaborate plan. Was it kindness or manipulation? Revenge, just like

Wanlapa had warned?

"Can I speak with you alone?" Mom Rapeekorn asked gently, turning to Phonpol for permission.

"I've got nothing to say," Shinakal blurted out before his friend could respond. *Don't leave me with him*, he begged silently. But Phonpol, clueless traitor that he was, stepped out and left them alone. Mom Rapeekorn didn't waste the opportunity. He shut the door and stepped closer.

"What did Wanlapa tell you?" the prince asked, his voice low but authoritative. Shinakal didn't want to answer. But that tone made resistance pointless. Like a prisoner finally cornered.

"She said… You might be my karmic retribution. Here to take revenge from a past life."

"I thought you didn't believe in any of that," Mom Rapeekorn said, gently taking his shoulder to make him face him.

"I didn't say that. I just… haven't made up my mind," Shinakal muttered, pouting.

"I've tried to tell you the truth so many times, but you never wanted to listen."

"Because everything you say sounds insane. Who has a third eye that sees the past and rewrites the future?"

"You ignored me every time I tried. But when Wanlapa says it once, you believe her?" Mom Rapeekorn bit his lip, eyes narrowing like he was scolding a stubborn child.

"I didn't believe her either! That's why I'm going home!" Shinakal snapped, backing up to the edge of the bed, away from Mom Rapeekorn's scent, away from those long fingers that might sneak a playful pinch again and ruin his resolve.

They sat in silence for a while. Until finally, Mom Rapeekorn sat down beside him.

"Is there anything you want to ask me?" he offered, calm and composed.

"How do I know if what you tell me is true?"

"And how do you know it's false if you never ask?"

Classic. A question answered with another question. Shinakal scowled at him.

"Fine. Then tell me. Why did you buy Grandpa Thien's house?"

"I've told you. I wanted to preserve it," Mom Rapeekorn said evenly.

"Liar. There are tons of old houses in need of saving. Grandpa Thien's house isn't even that special compared to others. Why that one?" Shinakal barked, raising his voice.

As expected, Mom Rapeekorn said nothing. He always went quiet when Shinakal yelled. Taking advantage of that silence, Shinakal jumped up and yanked his suitcase back out.

With a sigh, Mom Rapeekorn finally replied.

"Because it was your house."

There it was. Confirmation. Everything Wanlapa said, everything Shinakal suspected. It wasn't a coincidence. This man had followed him on purpose.

"Why me? And don't give me that love-at-first-sight crap. You didn't even know me."

"Have you ever heard of the Ayutthaya treasure?" Mom Rapeekorn asked, and Shinakal went cold without knowing why.

"I've heard bits and pieces."

"They say it was buried long ago so that only the rightful soul or their descendant could retrieve it. If someone unworthy tries to claim it, they'll be cursed."

Shinakal had read about it once in a magazine. He'd never paid it much mind. He wasn't from Ayutthaya. It's not like he was going to stumble into a moat and trip over royal jewels. Still, he didn't argue. He just walked back to sit at the writing desk, far enough from Mom Rapeekorn. Not because he didn't trust Mom Rapeekorn's hands—but because he didn't trust his own.

"After King Taksin drove the Burmese out and declared independence, he ordered both Thai and Chinese citizens to search for the hidden royal treasure. There was an official plan for dividing whatever was found between the palace and the people. But unofficially, secret groups were formed. They passed down the knowledge of how to find the treasure through generations. And what they really wanted was to find the rightful heir. Someone who could open the vaults without triggering a curse."

"The more you talk, the less I understand. What does this

have to do with me?" Shinakal shook his head. He felt like he and Mom Rapeekorn were living in two different centuries. Then came the whisper.

"Because you might be that rightful heir."

Chapter 15

Shinakal clutched his suitcase tightly, fingers stiff with tension. His eyes swept across the darkness pressing in from both sides of the road. The world outside was silent, consumed by shadow. Only a few scattered streetlamps flickered dimly along the roadside, casting long, trembling beams across the cracked asphalt. Beside him, Mom Rapheekorn kept his hands steady on the wheel, his gaze fixed ahead. He hadn't spoken a word since they left, his silence sharper than any warning.

This was the final stretch of the backroads. If they could make it past here, they would reach the main highway. From there, the way to Bangkok would be clearer, safer. But the quiet didn't last.

Two motorcycles surged out of the darkness, one on each

side of the car. Their engines snarled low, like a threat barely held in check. The riders wore police uniforms, but their movements were too practiced, too coordinated. One of them motioned for the car to pull over.

Mom Rapheekorn kept driving, his jaw tight and focused. The rider on the left moved in closer, matching their speed with unnerving precision. He gestured again, signaling for them to stop.

Mom Rapheekorn found the safest spot along the roadside and pulled over, but kept the engine running. "Is there a problem?" he asked, lowering the window just enough to let the voices through.

"We received a report that this car was stolen," the man in uniform said flatly. "I need both of you to step out of the vehicle."

"This car belongs to me," The car owner's voice was calm but commanding. "May I see your police identification first?"

"Step out of the car and I'll show you," the man replied, sounding far too casual.

"I think it's better if I verify you first. If you're really an officer, I will not resist. I have documents proving this vehicle is mine. I know I'm not a thief. The question is, are you really a cop?"

At that, the man in uniform exchanged a glance with his partner. Without a word, the second man stepped forward, pulled out a gun, and aimed it directly at them.

"Mom, watch out!" Shinakal shouted just as a bullet shattered the rear window.

Mom Rapheekorn slammed the accelerator. The car surged forward as he swerved to avoid the impostors. Their only focus now was reaching the main road before the next shot was fired.

"How did you know they were planning an ambush?" Shinakal shouted, panic tightening his voice. Before he could get a response, another gunshot cracked through the air. He ducked instinctively, his heart pounding in his chest.

Mom Rapeekorn tore down the narrow road, fields stretching endlessly on both sides. No one had known they were heading back to Bangkok. They hadn't told a soul. Not a message.

Not even a phone call that might have raised suspicion.

"Do you believe me now? Someone is trying to kill you," Mom Rapeekorn shouted, voice strained over the roar of the engine. The shattered rear window let in a rush of wind and noise from outside.

"I believe you!" Shinakal called back. For a moment, he had feared that Mom Rapeekorn was the danger. Now he knew the truth. They had almost died together.

Mom Rapeekorn's car shot forward at full speed. It might have been turbocharged. One of the motorcycles managed to catch up and began closing in. Mom Rapeekorn swerved hard, clipping it just enough to send it off the edge of the road. The second rider faltered as his partner went down, but continued the chase. He stayed on their tail until they were nearly at the highway, then suddenly veered off, unwilling to risk getting caught in open traffic.

When the road finally cleared and no pursuers remained, Mom Rapeekorn eased off the accelerator. The engine growled back into control. He glanced over at Shinakal, who sat hunched against the seat, eyes wide and still trembling from the close call.

"Don't worry. They weren't trying to kill you. If they wanted you dead, you'd be in a ditch by now," Mom Rapeekorn said with an infuriatingly calm smile, as if they'd just taken a wrong turn on the way to brunch.

"Oh, perfect. That makes me feel so much better," Shinakal snapped. "Truly. Deep inner peace achieved."

How could he even smile at a time like this? That calm, unbothered face. It wasn't just ice. It was polished granite with a driver's license.

"So... what now?" Shinakal muttered, voice still shaky.

"Do you still want to drive home tonight, or shall we circle back to the villa?" Mom Rapheekorn asked, casually checking the rearview mirror.

No one knew they had left. Shinakal hadn't told a soul, and Mom Rapeekornhadn't made any calls either. He had only said he wanted to prove that making the trip to Bangkok alone wouldn't be safe.

Well... Shinakal believed him now. "Let's go back to Bangkok. I'll call Phon and apologize later." Phonphol probably already knew he wanted to go home. He hadn't even tried to hide the way he sighed every few minutes, or how he kept zoning out while the two ladies talked and laughed like he wasn't there.

Being a third wheel in someone else's moment was tiring. He had smiled when expected, nodded when necessary, but deep down, he just wanted to leave. Phonphol usually noticed things like that. Still, Shinakal figured it would be better to call and explain later once they arrived in Bangkok. Knowing his friend, Phonphol would understand. He usually did. If he found out that Shinakal had left with Mom Rapheekorn, it probably wouldn't matter so long as he made it home safe.

"There's just one thing I still don't get," Shinakal said, his voice low. "How did they know I'm the one who can unlock the treasure? Was it because I put Grandpa Thian's house up for sale?" He had gone over everything Mom Rapheekorn had told him, again and again. But that part still didn't add up.

"Yes… and no," Mom Rapeekornsaid quietly, his voice barely more than a breath. "The truth is, they've been watching me for a long time. They always knew that one day, you and I were meant to cross paths."

***

Mom Rapheekorn had driven him home. It was already almost morning, and asking him to leave now would've been rude. After everything he had done, Shinakal couldn't bring himself to kick the man out into the dark.

"You can stay the night, Mom," Shinakal said. "I'll take the sofa."

The idea of sharing a bed was… no. Just no. Too close. Too dangerous.

"Thank you, but I'll sleep on the sofa," Mom Rapheekorn replied. "I don't want to steal your bed."

"No way. You've been driving for hours. You must be exhausted. Go ahead and rest. I slept a little in the car anyway. I'm not that tired." This would've sounded a lot more convincing if he hadn't yawned immediately after saying it.

He tried to cover it up, but it was too late. His face turned red as he caught the slight smirk on Mom Rapheekorn's face. The look in his eyes clearly said, Caught you.

"I slept on the sofa last time, too," Mom Rapeekorn

added.

"I… don't remember. What did I do that night?" Shinakal avoided looking at him.

"You pulled me onto the bed. Told me to sleep there with you. Once you passed out, I went back to the sofa."

So that dream where he thought he'd spent the night cuddling a man who smelled way too good, wasn't a dream? Shinakal turned bright red. Even if he couldn't remember it clearly, hearing it out loud was more than enough.

"I seriously don't remember. Let's blame the alcohol. That wasn't me, okay? That was drunk-Shinakal, who just jumped out the window in shame and promised never to come back."

Mom Rapheekorn let out a soft laugh. That was the thing about him. No matter how ridiculous Shinakal got, he never made it worse. Never teased too hard. Never looked down on him.

He just smiled. And somehow, that made everything harder to ignore.

However, unlike those fairy-tale romances where two

souls are bound by fate, some couples might truly be meant for each other, destined from a past life. But whatever this was between Shinakal and Mom Rapheekorn, it didn't feel like destiny. It felt more like chaos wearing a charming disguise.

***

The morning after, following a slightly awkward breakfast at his go-to café with Mom Rapheekorn, Shinakal returned home only to get an earful from Phonphol. It was a long-winded scolding for leaving without saying goodbye. But honestly, if he had said goodbye, would he have been allowed to leave at all?

Meanwhile, Mom Rapeekorn was waiting on the sofa, freshly showered and smelling like he'd just stepped out of a spa. He had brought a change of clothes from their trip to Phetchaburi and now looked perfectly at ease.

"May I read Grandpa Thian's diary?" he asked, picking up the thread from their conversation the night before. Shinakal had already mentioned that he kept it here.

"Sure. I'll go get it," Shinakal replied, heading to the bedroom. He retrieved both the diary and the letters from where he had hidden them in the wardrobe. But just as Mom Rapeekorn was about to open it, Shinakal spoke up again.

"Before you read it… can you explain something to me? How do you know things? The past. The future. All of it."

Mom Rapheekorn didn't look the least bit uncomfortable. It was as if he had been expecting the question all along.

"My grandfather used to consult a book called The Treatise of Victory in War before doing anything important. Whether it was opening a business or starting a project, he'd always read it first. At the time, I assumed it was something like The Art of War, a book on military tactics, strategy, that sort of thing. But when I finally read it for myself, I realized it wasn't that at all. It was about astrology. About reading the stars, the sky, the winds and how those things could guide your path. After that, I started noticing things. Places, objects… they don't just sit quietly. Most of them hold on to a memory and some feeling. Thais might call it a spirit. Westerners, who don't believe in such things, would probably call it memory instead. But it's the same presence."

"You can see the past just by touching objects?"

Mom Rapeekorn didn't reply with words. He simply nodded slowly, perhaps afraid that saying too much would make him sound like he was showing off some kind of supernatural ability.

"And the part where you knew someone would try to hurt me. How did you know that?"

"The Treatise is about interpreting numbers and timing. When you celebrated your birthday, I used your birth date to do a reading. That's how I saw the danger coming."

"Isn't that a bit creepy, Mom? You took my birthdate and then showed up at my house uninvited." Shinakal recalled a warning written in Grandpa Thian's diary. Never reveal your birthdate to anyone.

If Grandpa Thian had known Facebook existed, where everyone's birthday is public, he'd probably faint every day.

"You can call it whatever you like. All I know is, I didn't want you to get hurt. They followed me until they found you. And now it's my duty to protect you."

That was another matter entirely. Shinakal didn't know

whether he should be angry at Mom Rapeekorn for bringing danger to his doorstep or grateful that he kept saving his life.

"May I read the diary now?" Mom Rapeekorn asked calmly, raising an eyebrow.

"Do you want the Ayutthaya treasure too?"

"The treasure isn't mine to claim. Keeping it would only bring misfortune. What about you? Do you plan to dig it up?" He answered without hesitation, as if the thought had never once tempted him. But there was a glint of disappointment in his eyes. No matter how much he had done to prove himself, Shinakal still didn't completely trust him.

They stared at each other for a long moment, until Shinakal finally stepped forward and handed him the diary.

"I don't know what they're really after," he said. "I've read the diary, but I still haven't found any mention of the treasure you're talking about."

Mom Rapeekorn placed the diary flat on the table, then took out a notebook and pen. He began jotting down the dates written inside, as if he were trying to uncover hidden patterns rather than simply reading for meaning.

***

Phonphol and Saiparn had been downstairs since eight. Breakfast was laid out, the morning sun already sharp, and the coffee had gone cold by the time the clock neared nine. But Wanlapa was still nowhere to be seen. Phonphol stabbed the last sausage on his plate and popped it into his mouth, then tilted his head toward Saiparn's untouched plate. She'd been poking at the sausage on it for twenty minutes, lost in thought.

"Can I have it?" he asked sweetly. It sounded more like a proposal than a request. He leaned in a little too close for comfort.

"Hey, back off," Saiparn said, pushing his face away. "No one's watching anymore." Her father's spy and Phonphol's friend had both returned to Bangkok yesterday. In theory, they should have had some peace. Time to unwind. Maybe even talk.

They'd thought they'd finally get to spend time with Wanlapa, just the three of them. But ever since they arrived, Miss Fancy had locked herself in her room. She was the one who had insisted on this trip in the first place. And now she refused to go

248

anywhere, complaining that the sun was too strong, that she didn't want her skin to burn. And just when Saiparn was about to knock on her door for the third time, Wanlapa finally emerged with her suitcase in hand.

"Parn, I'm really sorry," she said, hands in a wai, voice small and sugar-coated in that overly cute tone she used whenever she wanted something. "My manager just called. Something urgent came up. I have to get back to Bangkok. Like, right now."

"You're kidding me," Saiparn snapped. Her face flushed with irritation. "You told me you cleared your whole schedule."

"I did. But this just came up. Orders from above. I seriously can't say no. You and Phon go ahead, okay? If I finish early, I'll come right back. There's still time left on the trip, right?"

Phonphol frowned. Something about her felt… off. But he said nothing. In his mind, the gods of fate had just given him one-on-one time with Saiparn.

"We're not staying without you," Saiparn said flatly.

"What? But I don't want to leave yet," Phonphol cut in.

"Then stay. Alone." Saiparn's glare could have set fire to the tablecloth. Why were tomboys so good at that?

Wanlapa tried one last time. "If we all go back now, won't your dad get suspicious? Just stay a little longer, please. I promise I'll come back soon."

She kissed Saiparn on the cheek. "You believe me, right?"

Saiparn's face softened, her eyes wide with emotion. "You really mean it?"

Phonphol slammed his hand on his knee. Why doesn't anyone ever look at me like that?

"Well then… how are you getting back?" he asked.

"I hired a car. It's already outside." She pointed toward the front gate. A silver Toyota idled quietly in the driveway. As she approached, a man in sunglasses stepped out and loaded her suitcase into the trunk without a word.

Wanlapa slipped into the passenger seat. The door shut. Moments later, the man beside her gave a quiet report.

"He's with Mom now."

Wanlapa didn't answer right away. She looked back at the

bungalow, where Phonphol and Saiparn still stood at the doorway, both looking confused, still not entirely sure what had just happened.

Chapter 16

Shinakal had dozed off with the TV remote still in his hand. He didn't know how long he'd been out, but when he looked around, he saw Mom Rapheekorn, who had earlier been poring over Grandpa Thian's documents with deep concentration, now slumped over the stack of letters, head resting against them.

Shinakal stood there watching him sleep, unsure whether he should wake him or not. After all, his guest hadn't slept much, unlike him, who at least got some rest during the drive since he didn't have to be the one driving.

"Mom… why don't you sleep in my room? It'll be more comfortable." His condo only had one bedroom, and he rarely had anyone stay over. It wasn't spacious. And when someone did spend the night, it was usually someone who was invited to sleep in the same bed. Mom Rapheekorn looked toward the window, checking the morning light, then quietly began gathering the documents spread out on the desk.

"I'll help pack them up," Shinakal offered. "You go ahead and lie down." The letters were already organized by date. All that was left was to box them up.

"It's alright. I just need to wash my face a bit," Mom Rapheekorn mumbled, pointing toward the bathroom. Shinakal nodded, still a little worried. He knew the guest was eager to finish decoding Grandpa Thian's secrets, and for good reason, his entire mission hinged on it.

"Would you like a toothbrush? I have extras," he offered after hearing the water running. "You could also shower, if you like. I'll get you a towel."

"Thank you," came the voice from behind the door.

Shinakal sprinted off to grab one of the towels he had bought long ago and never got a chance to use. Like he'd somehow always known someone would come visit. Was it fate? He'd washed and folded the towel, tucked it away neatly, waiting for this moment. He grabbed it and returned to knock gently on the bathroom door. It opened!

And he nearly passed out. Figuratively speaking, of course. Because Mom Rapeekorn wore only his pants, unhooked and just barely hanging on to those hips.

Was he doing this on purpose?!

"Um… here." Shinakal offered the towel, his hand frozen midair. His eyes accidentally dipped too low, landing right where a tempting V-line and thick hair peeked above the waistband. They say hairy men are hungry beasts.

Dangerous. Strong. Sexy. *Look away, Shin! Look away!*

"You're staring," Mom Rapeekorn said, amused, like he knew exactly what he was doing.

"Then stop being so damn hot." A snap comeback. Sure, he always called people perverts. Turns out, he was into perverts, too. Hypocritical much? When Shinakal still hadn't handed the towel over, Mom Rapeekorn had to reach out and take it himself. But to do that, he had to step in closer. Just one step. That's all it took in this tiny bathroom.

Suddenly, his abs, softly dusted with hair, were pressing

right up against Shinakal.

He looked up, breath caught in his throat. The room dimmed. But it wasn't from fainting. It was from the blinding spark that burst behind his eyes as soon as Mom Rapeekorn leaned in and kissed him. Shinakal didn't even remember who kissed who first. A kiss is a kiss. And this one? It was a damn good one. Not too wet, not too dry. Just soft, warm, and perfect. Mom Rapeekorn pressed Shinakal gently against the doorframe, hands firm on his shoulders. This time, Shinakal was sure it was Mom Rapeekorn who started it. Hands and all. So he took the chance to undo the last piece of clothing, letting those half-hung pants fall to the floor. The advantage was his. Mom Rapeekorn was naked. He wasn't—yet. Even though Mom Rapeekorn was definitely working on it, at least this time, he wouldn't be left standing there high and dry like before.

"Is this where you kill me after sex, like in some stalker thriller?" Shinakal asked breathlessly.

"I told you, I'm not a stalker. I just read your fortune and followed you in time to stop a robbery. But even if I explain it, you wouldn't believe me."

"No need to explain anymore, Mom. Just take your clothes off and prove your intentions," he quipped.

Typical Shin. Can't help but be cheeky, even when facing possible murder. Mom Rapeekorn smiled, fingers slipping under his shirt, undoing the buttons one by one. Then he leaned in close and whispered in a tone that made Shinakal's knees buckle.

"Take off your pants."

And what did the dumb little frog prince do? He obeyed. His bare butt wobbled its way right into the arms of a real-life blueblood. Mom Rapeekorncame here to buy the house, but now it looked like he'd taken ownership of its owner, too. Buy one, get one free. Win-win for both buyer and seller.

Fully undressed, Shinakal walked over to the bed and casually peeled off his cartoon-print tee. No underwear, no shame.

"Condoms are in the right drawer. Lube on the left. Tissues in the back."

He said it like he'd rehearsed it like a pro. But Mom Rapeekorn didn't even go for the drawer. He just kissed him again, silencing him with soft, plump lips, moving slowly down his neck, then his chest, then lower.

Shinakal's little friend stood so proudly that it might as well have saluted. Calm down, little guy! At least pretend to have some shame. His brain begged for control, but his hips had a mind of their own, lifting instinctively as Mom's mouth wrapped around him like silk.

Lips, tongue, warmth, depth. Shinakal had been afraid old-fashioned noble types wouldn't know how to do this sort of thing. He was wrong. Not only did Mom Rapeekorn know, he was dangerously good at it.

And you know what?

If this is how I die, then let me die by the mouth of a royal killer. At least my corpse would look cute, all flushed and pink and respectable.

***

It was the first time Shinakal had ever woken up and actually gotten to lie there, watching the face of the man he'd just slept with. Morning sunlight filtered gently through the curtain folds, casting a soft glow over Mom Rapeekorn's resting features. Every other time in his life, Shinakal had either been the one passed out, lost to drink, or simply woken to an empty bed and the chill of absence. But this morning felt different. Stillness had never felt this full before. And the best part…he was still alive and well!!!

"Why are you staring?" Mom Rapeekorn murmured without opening both eyes, only one eye peeking up with mild curiosity. He reached up, hand warm and steady, and drew Shinakal gently down until their foreheads nearly touched. Then came a soft kiss pressed to Shinakal's brow, gentle as silk, affectionate in a way that caught him off guard. It felt almost paternal, and yet somehow made his heart flutter.

"I was just thinking," Shinakal said softly, "You're the first one I've woken up with still lying next to me." Mom Rapeekorn raised an eyebrow, questioning without speaking. Shinakal smiled faintly. "Most of the others panic. Or they sneak out before I wake up. I guess they never really meant to be there."

"Why?" Mom Rapeekorn asked, voice low, still caught between waking and dream.

"Maybe it was one of those oops moments. The kind people like to pretend it didn't happen. You know. Just one wild night, the mood carried them away. It's never like the novels where someone stays to cook breakfast or even say goodbye." He laughed quietly to himself, not bitter but knowing. "But you're still here. And that's new."

"This isn't an oops moment for me. I'm just not sure I have the energy to make breakfast." Mom Rapeekorn reached for the bedside clock, checked the time, and stretched slowly beneath the sheets. "Can I take you out to eat instead? Although I suppose it's a bit late for porridge." He paused, then glanced at Shinakal's phone charging on the table. "Oh…check your bank account."

Shinakal frowned but reached for it. A few swipes later, his eyes widened. "Ten million baht? What the—"

"Don't worry. It's not a payment for services rendered," Mom Rapeekorn said, amused. "It's the deposit for the house. I've spoken to Mr. Phon already. We'll transfer the rest on the day we sign."

"Oh," Shinakal exhaled with relief. "For a second, I thought I'd just been mistaken for an expensive escort."

Mom Rapeekorn chuckled again, slipping one hand beneath his head. "You can buy breakfast, then. Your staff's been paid for the month."

"In that case, let me take you somewhere nice. Maybe seafood by the sea?" He couldn't tell if Mom Rapeekorn was joking or serious, but if it was seafood by the sea, that would practically be a date.

He wanted to ask what they were now, what this moment between them meant. But the words caught behind his teeth. Maybe it was better to let it linger like this. Undefined. Unhurried. After all, Mom Rapeekorn was still here, and the house deal was real.

They ended up at a rooftop buffet, the kind that usually needed a week's advance booking. Yet somehow, Mom Rapeekorn just walked in with him and was shown straight to the VIP section like it was nothing. Shinakal, who'd never eaten in a place that high, stared at the view and then at the man across from him with silent awe.

"Working in the ministry pays that well?" he asked. "Enough to buy houses and get private tables without reservations? Are you sure you're a civil servant and not a politician?" He nearly added mafia boss, but decided against it.

Best not to get kicked out of his own date.

"I also do real estate and hold shares in a few companies. Just enough to live comfortably," Mom Rapeekorn answered nonchalantly.

A few companies. Shinakal sighed internally. Dividend life must be something else.

As they walked to the buffet line, Mom Rapeekorn poured a glass of wine and returned with it in hand, his eyes more serious now.

"I read your grandfather's diary again last night. There's no mention of the pendant. But one thing still bothers me. No one ever talks about Princess Praphaiphon. There's not even a photo of her in the house."

"I don't know much either. Grandpa Thian brought Grandpa Udom to live in that house alone. Princess Praphaiphon never moved in."

"Does anyone know where she went?"

"My dad might. When Grandpa Udom passed away, someone from the Narathip family sent a wreath. And Dad once told me Grandpa used to take him to visit her."

"I see. Would you mind calling him? Ask if this address is the Narathip residence." Mom Rapeekorn took out a pen and gently wrote the address across Shinakal's palm.

Shinakal squinted, then nodded and made the call. When he hung up, his face had lost its playful ease.

"How did you know that?" he asked quietly.

"I thought I mentioned it. I see spirits sometimes. If someone near me is thinking about someone, or talking about them, their spirit can appear. Sometimes they say something. Sometimes they don't."

"Is she… here?" Shinakal waved the air beside him nervously.

"She was," Mom Rapeekorn replied, smiling. "She's gone now."

Shinakal stared at his palm again. It was hard to believe, but harder still to argue with what he'd just experienced. That address. That name. Nothing had ever been recorded about Princess Praphaiphon, not in the diary, not anywhere. He had only found out from the letter that his grandfather had been married before.

"You're planning to investigate her, aren't you?"

"If you're free, I'd like you to come with me," Mom Rapeekorn said gently. "We might find a clue about the pendant. And why are so many people desperate to find it?"

Shinakal nodded.

Chapter 17

They didn't bother with a long drive—flying to Phitsanulok took less than an hour and was far more convenient. After landing, Mom Rapeekorn rented a car and drove them toward the quiet district where the old Narathip House stood.

Waiting at the entrance was a poised woman, about the same age as Mom Rapeekorn. She introduced herself as Phichaya Thongmak, a granddaughter of the princess. Curiously, however, she didn't carry Grandfather Thian's surname.

The current owner of the Narathip House brought out Butterfly pea flower juice and Bulan Dan Mek, a delicate, old-fashioned royal dessert made with the same blossoms.

"I know this dessert," Shinakal said with a hint of surprise. "Grandpa Udom used to make it for me. He said it was a fortune-telling dessert from the palace."

Phichaya's face lit up, her eyes sparkling as if she were reconnecting with a long-lost friend.

"Yes," she said warmly. "My great-grandmother brought the recipe from the royal court. She used to pray before steaming it, then wait to see whether the top turned out round and beautiful like the moon. They say she once prayed that she'd get to marry my great-grandfather."

"Your great-grandfather… was he Grandfather Thian?" Shinakal asked, hesitant. His father had never mentioned any relatives in this part of the country. But from the way Phichaya spoke, it seemed she truly was the princess's direct descendant.

"Oh no," Phichaya replied with an easy smile, as if it were no unusual thing. "My great-grandmother was married twice."

Shinakal raised his brows. No one had ever told him anything about Princess Praphaiphon's past—not even that she had once been married to Grandfather Thian.

"I was fortunate," Phichaya went on. "My great-grandmother lived a long life, and her memory stayed sharp. She loved telling stories about Grandfather Thian. She said that the moment she saw him, she fell in love. But he already carried someone else in his heart. Later, to help save him from danger, Prince Khun Luang requested a royal arrangement for her to marry him. Since she already loved him in secret, she accepted. But theirs was only a marriage in name."

Smiling, Phichaya offered Shinakal another piece of the moon-shaped dessert, then continued.

"Later, when Grandfather Thian was preparing to move to Bangkok, he asked her if she wanted to go with him. But she declined. Instead, she ended up marrying my great-grandfather, who, incidentally, had once been Grandfather Thian's student." She tilted her head in thought, then laughed fondly at the memory. "She was a bit of a firecracker. She liked to joke that eating 'tender grass'—her own cheeky term for younger men—would help her live longer. And yes, she said it with a straight face."

At that, both Mom Rapeekorn and Shinakal burst into laughter. They couldn't picture the real Princess Praphaiphon, but the thought of her brought a strange warmth.

"She must have been quite the character," Shinakal said. "It's a shame I never got the chance to meet her."

"She used to talk about your Grandpa Udom all the time. You do know that Her Highness was the one who raised him since he was a baby, don't you?"

"I do," Shinakal nodded. "Grandpa always said he was a child she took in and raised as her own."

"Oh, and there's one more thing my great-grandmother left in my care," Phichaya said, as if just remembering something. She hurried over to a drawer and pulled out a silver box, handing it to Shinakal.

"After Prince Khun Luang passed away, my great-grandfather—the Princess's father—found this box in the old palace at Sra Bua Canal. He recognized it immediately. Said he'd once seen Grandfather Thian wearing it. So he entrusted it to Her Highness, asking her to keep it safe until it could be returned to its rightful owner." Phichaya gently placed the ornate silver box in Shinakal's hands. Her voice softened.

"My great-grandmother told me she tried to give it back

many times. But he always refused. Perhaps he thought it safer this way. But for me, keeping it here has been a quiet burden. I've always feared that one day his descendants might come looking and I'd have nothing left to give."

Shinakal opened the box with reverent fingers.

Inside lay a golden pendent, its surface inlaid with rich enamel, gleaming beneath the dim afternoon light. At the top rose a delicate lotus bud, shaped like a royal prang, just as Grandfather Thian had described in his old letter.

His breath caught. Eyes wide with disbelief, he turned to Mom Rapeekorn.

This was it. The missing piece. The secret pendant.

"What is lost, if it's truly yours, will always find its way back to you." The words from the diary rang clear in his mind.

***

He had found it at last! The infamous pendant.

"What should we do next?" Shinakal clutched the box as if it might vanish again.

"We see whether the treasure mentioned in the diary is

real," Mom Rapeekorn replied as he drove. The diary described the way to unlock the cache and the exact location where the treasure was buried. Yet Grandpa Thian had never allowed anyone to dig it up, not even Prince Khun Luang himself.

"Are you actually going to unearth it?" Shinakal asked, uncertain.

"If we don't, we'll never know if the treasure exists, will we? Besides, the people after you aren't going to stop unless someone proves that the treasure's already been found or that it doesn't exist."

Shinakal's heart thudded anxiously. He wasn't sure whether he should get involved at all. "I heard there's some complicated ritual involved," he added.

"We just need manpower. Ayutthaya isn't far. I've got a few contacts there. We could call in a few favors. Shouldn't be too difficult."

True enough, it wasn't even sunset by the time their rental car pulled into a modest hotel in Ayutthaya. Mom Rapeekorn made a few quick, quiet calls. Within minutes, two young men arrived, clad in black T-shirts and khaki work pants, with the silent alertness of soldiers. They looked like conscripts, but Mom Rapeekorn introduced them as local ministry staff.

They came in a double-cab pickup truck, dust-streaked and worn. One opened the rear door for Shinakal without a word. Mom Rapeekorn took the passenger seat. The other man hopped into the truck bed, guarding a set of digging tools—shovels, pickaxes, and a canvas bag whose contents clinked ominously. By the time they reached Wat Chaiwatthanaram, it was still shy of midnight. The ancient temple stood shrouded in shadow, its chedis and spires casting long, haunting silhouettes against the night sky. Yet no one moved to dig. Not yet. They waited. For what, Shinakal didn't know.

Nearly two hours passed. The silence of the sleeping village settled thick and heavy. Until the low rumble of engines pierced it. Headlights cut across the courtyard as two more vehicles approached: a black sedan and another pickup truck, unmarked, dust trailing behind them like ghosts. Shinakal turned, uneasy.

"Are they with you?" he began to ask. But the words died in his throat.

The Toyota's door opened with a click that echoed too loudly in the stillness. And out stepped Wanlapa.

She didn't speak. She didn't smile. She simply raised a pistol and leveled it at his chest.

"What's going on, Mom?" Shinakal asked, noticing how casually Mom Rapeekorngreeted them as if he knew them well. Before he could get an answer, one of Wanlapa's men slapped handcuffs on him and shoved him toward the base of the central prang.

"Told you not to trust him," Wanlapa said smugly. The man who handcuffed Shinakal wasn't a stranger. He was the fake cop who had stopped him on the road in Phetchaburi just the other night. The same one now shoved him hard, nearly smashing his face into the dirt.

"Hey! Easy. I told you not to hurt him," Mom Rapeekorn snapped. His voice was suddenly stern and sharp, a far cry from the smooth tones Shinakal had grown used to.

"What is this?" Shinakal demanded again as the man came to stand beside him.

"Don't worry, they won't hurt you. Once we open the vault, we'll split the treasure and return to Bangkok."

"Split what?"

"If the treasure is real, everyone gets a share, and we go our separate ways," Mom Rapeekorn said coolly, not even blinking.

So that was it. He wasn't a government officer. He was worse. A scavenger. A traitor. A treasure thief.

"Is this your real estate business? You're not buying and selling homes. You're digging up a national treasure!" Shinakal shouted, enraged. How could he have been so foolish? All that talk about knowing the past and future. It was all a lie. Mom Rapeekornhad access to everything because he was one of them. Phonpol had suspected this. He should have listened. He should never have let a handsome face lead him this far astray.

"Shut it," the fake cop hissed. "Unless you want real cops showing up."

What kind of madness was this?

"Treasure buried underground is worthless until it's

unearthed," Mom Rapeekorn said, infuriatingly smug. "At least then, future generations might get to see it."

Shinakal wanted to bite his ear off. But for now, he had no choice but to go along with it. Wait for the right moment. Escape. Or call the police later.

Mom Rapeekorn laid the ritual tools, exactly as described in the diary, before the temple hall. No white-robed Brahmin this time. He would lead the chant himself. The golden pendant was set before Shinakal. Then someone kicked the back of his knee, forcing him to kneel.

"I promise," Mom Rapeekorn said, voice soft again, "if you cooperate, they won't harm you. And once it's over, I'll marry you. We'll be together." He leaned in for a kiss.

"I don't want to marry a thief!" Shinakal turned his face away.

Who would want to kiss someone who sold out their country? Just the memory of sleeping with him now made Shinakal sick. A flash of déjà vu: Grandpa Thian, sitting in this exact spot. Being forced to say those words. Now it was Shinakal's turn.

As he spoke the words aloud, an elephant's cry echoed in the distance. But this time, there was no escape.

The ground trembled slightly when Mom Rapeekorn's chant ended. A brilliant light rose from the north side of the prang. He nodded to the diggers, who moved to the glowing spot and began to dig. No trumpet of war elephants like in the diary. Everything unfolded as the treasure hunters had planned.

Shinakal bowed his head as they dug into the sacred earth. When they reached a layer of gleaming sand, Mom Rapeekorn raised his hands and chanted again. Maybe this was why Grandpa Thian had never claimed the pendant. He knew the treasure would fall into the wrong hands.

Maybe what Wanlapa had said was true. The prince had come back to get revenge. Maybe now their karmic debts were paid in full. Please, let me never meet him again in the next life.

"I hate you more than anyone," Shinakal whispered, tears running freely down his cheeks. This was heartbreak.

"Found the cave entrance!" one of the diggers shouted. And then a blinding pain in the neck. Something hard struck him from behind.

Khon Spy Behind the Fallen Prince

Darkness swallowed him whole. He wasn't sure if he was alive or dead. There were sirens. Flashing lights. A strong scent of incense that clung to his nose. Voices calling his name over and over again.

"Khun Luang?" Shinakal called out. Just saying the name brought him calm.

A great elephant stepped forward and nudged him gently with its trunk, urging him to stand. Is this the same elephant Grandpa Thian wrote about? Where is it taking me?

Chapter 18

Why the hell did I even survive? Shinakal lay on the stiff hospital bed, glaring blankly at the TV screen as the evening news blared on. Police bust treasure-hunting gang in Ayutthaya. The headline crawled across the bottom. He didn't want to deal with any of it, so he grabbed the remote and shut it off like slapping down a mosquito.

The cops had already swarmed in right after he regained consciousness. Bombarded him with questions—Do you know Wanlapa? Were you involved? He'd said nothing. Couldn't, really. His brain was fogged out on painkillers, mouth dry, eyes swimming. Even if he'd wanted to deny it all, he couldn't. And what was there to deny?

There was a video of him checking into a hotel with Mom

Rapeekorn. Calm. Willing. No sign of coercion. No one had tied him up. No one had dragged him there by force. The facts didn't care about context.

The officers backed off once they saw he wasn't fit for questioning. They promised they'd be back. And his father had been at his bedside ever since. Watching. Saying nothing. Probably because he knew damn well that Shinakal wasn't ready to hear what he deserved to hear.

Idiot. Absolute idiot.

You let a man play you like a damn violin, and you still don't want to admit it.

A knock jolted him from his thoughts. Two sharp raps. Then the door opened without waiting for permission. Of course. Why would anyone wait these days? At least the guy had the sense to greet his father.

"Oh, hey, Phon. How are you?"

"All good, Uncle. Sorry, I only just heard Shinakal was in the hospital. I just got back from upcountry." His cheery face was more upbeat than usual, which irked Shinakal.

He hadn't answered a single call. Then yesterday, fresh from his mountain trip, Phonpol had posted a sappy photo of him kissing his tomboy girlfriend on top of a scenic cliff, captioned: "Mission: Turning Tomboy into Girlfriend." He even flashed a victory sign. Shinakal had responded with a middle finger emoji.

"You bastard! You ditched your friend the moment you got laid. Dumped me like trash," Shinakal was about to continue the tirade, but Phonpol quickly cut in.

"I'm here now, aren't I? And I brought the contract to transfer the house." He handed over a folder, reminding Shinakal of something important.

"Wait. Sign it with who? Isn't Mom in jail now?"

"Mom Rapeekorn, of course. He has already set the meeting. Should be here any minute." Phonpol glanced at his watch. Right on cue, a knock sounded again. This time, Phonpol practically bounced to the door and opened it with a big smile.

"Good afternoon, Khun Rapee."

Shinakal's jaw dropped. The man who should have been behind bars was now standing in the doorway, holding a bouquet of champaca blossoms. Somehow, he had strolled right past the police officer stationed outside the room.

What kind of connections does it take to walk free from a case of national heritage theft?

"Mom!" Shinakal sat bolt upright. That face—so handsome. And so shameless.

"What's with the look? You act like you've seen a ghost." Phonpol waved the folder of contracts in front of his friend's face.

"Uncle," Mom Rapeekorn said respectfully. "May I have a word alone with Shinakal?"

Taking the hint, Phonpol placed the documents on the table and stepped out with Shinakal's father.

"I don't know how you managed to walk out of jail, but I'll never forgive you, as for the house. Forget it. I'm not selling. I'll return your money. Just leave. I never want to see your face again."

Shinakal stared at him, fury in his eyes. Mom Rapeekorn didn't flinch. They held each other's gaze in tense silence until he finally spoke.

"I was the one who tipped off the police. That's why they were waiting at Wat Chaiwatthanaram. I've already testified that you were coerced and had no part in the illegal excavation."

"What… did you just say?" Shinakal blinked, unsure he heard right.

"They'd been looking for the owner of the pendant for a long time. I had to use it as bait to lure them out. I knew Wanlapa was one of them, so I pretended to be on her side, promised to hand over the ornament and split the treasure. That gave me the chance to bring the police in and catch them all. If you'd watched the news, you'd know they got every last one, including the bastard who bashed your head in."

As he finished speaking, Mom Rapeekorn stepped closer to inspect the wound on the back of Shinakal's head. A fractured skull, the doctor had said. Not too serious, but they still needed to monitor for swelling. If all went well, he'd be discharged soon.

"So… where's the treasure now?" Shinakal still wasn't entirely convinced. Handsome men were the worst deceivers.

"All the recovered artifacts are currently on display at the Fine Arts Department. I think it's a good thing they were unearthed—those relics are reminders of a time when Thailand was at its cultural peak. A time of unity, before division and conflict weakened our defenses and led to our downfall."

Shinakal looked at Mom Rapeekorn. For the first time, he truly saw him as royal. Not just by blood, but by heart. A man who loved his country deeply. Then again, everyone expresses patriotism differently.

"So you really weren't a treasure-hunting mafia boss?" Instead of replying, Mom Rapeekorn leaned in and kissed his forehead.

Shinakal tilted his head up, expecting a kiss on the lips. Their mouths met gently.

Then he asked, "What about that promise you made—to marry me? Was that real or just sweet talk?"

Mom Rapeekorn picked up the contract papers, signed his name with a flourish, and handed them back.

"Maybe we should change the name of that old house," he whispered into Shinakal's ear. "From Khun Luang's

Residence to Our Residence. What do you say?"

==The End==

www.ingramcontent.com/pod-product-compliance
Lightning Source LLC
Chambersburg PA
CBHW071545110726
47908CB00007B/1996